"Ms. Harper, Open Up! It's the Sheriff."

Limp with relief, Ellie rushed to open the door.

Ben Stapleton, wearing jeans and a cream-colored Windbreaker, looked down at her as she stood there in her robe, clutching a broom.

"Come in," she said breathlessly. "I heard that noise again a few minutes ago. It seemed to be coming from over there."

She looked up at him. He noted the receding fright in her dark eyes. Her auburn hair was mussed from sleep, and the white satin robe she wore revealed intriguing glimpses of her figure. She was an eyeful, all right.

Ben was fascinated.

JEANNE STEPHENS
loves to travel, but she's always glad to get home to her Oklahoma cattle ranch. This mother of three loves reading ("I'll read anything!" she says), needlework, photography and long walks, during which she works out her latest books.

Dear Reader:

Romance readers have been enthusiastic about Silhouette Special Editions for years. And that's not by accident: Special Editions were the first of their kind and continue to feature realistic stories with heightened romantic tension.

The longer stories, sophisticated style, greater sensual detail and variety that made Special Editions popular are the same elements that will make you want to read book after book.

We hope that you enjoy this Special Edition today, and will enjoy many more.

The Editors at Silhouette Books

JEANNE STEPHENS
Mandy's Song

Silhouette Special Edition
Published by Silhouette Books New York
America's Publisher of Contemporary Romance

SILHOUETTE BOOKS
300 E. 42nd St., New York, N.Y. 10017

Distributed by Pocket Books

ISBN: 0-373-09217-2

First Silhouette Books printing February, 1985

10 9 8 7 6 5 4 3 2 1

Map by Ray Lundgren

SILHOUETTE, SILHOUETTE SPECIAL EDITION and
colophon are registered trademarks of the publisher.

America's Publisher of Contemporary Romance

Printed in the U.S.A.

Mandy's Song

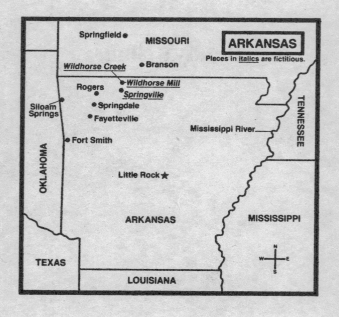

Chapter One

Ellie remembered the Ozarks from a few carefree summers spent visiting her grandparents after her father's death. As she drove on the narrow, twisting road through the outskirts of Springville, Arkansas, memories bombarded her: sleepy summer afternoons, heavy with silence broken only by the drowsy clicking of cicadas; cold spring water rippling along its rocky bed, so clear you could see the outline of every stone; exploring the wooded hills surrounding her grandparents' farm and returning, hot and tired, to drink from the tin dipper in the kitchen water bucket; nights of deep, dreamless slumber in the cot on the porch of the farmhouse.

When the bottom had dropped out of her life in

Houston, those childhood memories had surfaced like perfect diamonds working their way to the top of a sea of glass baubles, and Ellie had begun to think about coming back. Like returning to the womb, she thought. She might be disappointed, she told herself—she was trying not to expect miracles. Childhood's idyllic memories had a way of tarnishing like silver when exposed to adult scrutiny. She knew that she was grasping at straws, but she'd wanted to get out of Houston and retreating to the setting where she had been the happiest and most secure as a youngster was the best she could do right now.

The counselor she'd been seeing for the past several weeks had approved the journey. "Just don't make any irreversible decisions for a while," she'd said. "Think of it as a vacation. Give yourself time to heal. And don't be surprised if you overreact to people and situations at first. Your self-esteem is still pretty fragile and your emotions are very close to the surface."

Greg thought she'd gone mad, but then Greg hadn't understood her for years. She realized now that he probably never had; that had been as much her fault as his. To please him, she'd tried to become the person he wanted her to be . . . and had lost herself in the process.

She had to find herself again. She hadn't been alone since the age of twenty, and she had the sensation of having awakened from a nine-year sleep. The world had gone on without her. Greg had gone on. Now she had to step back into the world and make a place for the real Ellie who had become a stranger to Mrs. Greg Harper.

Sheriff Ben Stapleton inched his patrol car down Springville's congested main street. The place was bursting at the seams with tourists. The chamber of commerce had to count dogs and cats to come up with a population of three thousand during the winter months. With its narrow streets and limited parking spaces, Springville hadn't been designed to accommodate fifty thousand people at one time, which was the average number the chamber said descended upon it every day from May through October.

Ben had grown up in Springville before the area became one of the biggest tourist attractions in that part of the country. Now people came from all over the nation to enjoy the natural beauty of the Ozarks and to buy the native crafts for sale in dozens of tourist-season shops. They spent their evenings in the motels, restaurants, and country music showhouses that clustered on the outskirts of Springville.

Since the vast majority of Spring County's population lived in the town, the distinction between the city police and the sheriff's department was blurred. Within the city limits they shared some of the same responsibilities. Ben and his deputies were kept busy during the season breaking up drunken fights and parties that had gotten too loud and issuing tickets for traffic violations. The sheriff's department had already investigated a murder and several accidental killings, most of them the result of gunshot wounds from "unloaded" guns, and the season was hardly over, it was only the first week of September.

Ben was frequently reminded, at the weekly chamber of commerce luncheons, that the tourist trade was vital to the survival of local merchants, but he couldn't help wishing that Springville could return to what it had been when he was growing up, a slow-paced, rather isolated little village, the ideal place to raise kids. In fact, his reservations about the quality of life in his hometown had led him to buy a house ten miles outside the city limits where he retreated gratefully when he wasn't on duty.

The county road leading to his place was often congested with cars traveling to the old grist mill that a retired preacher from Missouri had restored and turned into another tourist attraction. But Ben's house was a mile beyond the mill, a six-room log cabin with pine paneling and exposed beams, nestled in the midst of five acres of woods and blissful quiet.

"I wish I were there right now," Ben muttered as he saw a yellow Mercedes glide through the red light at the south end of Main Street. The driver was alone, a woman. Cursing under his breath, he turned on his siren and as soon as there was a space in the traffic, made a U-turn and wheeled in behind the Mercedes.

The woman drew over into a loading zone in front of a furniture store and stopped. Texas plates, Ben noted as he climbed out of the patrol car and walked up to the Mercedes.

The window rolled down. She removed a pair of oversized sunglasses and looked up at him with luminous brown eyes wide in an expression of surprise.

"Yes?" The afternoon sun burnished copper highlights in auburn hair brushed in casual waves away from her face.

"I'll have to see your license, ma'am."

Sooty lashes came down to hide her dark eyes, and she didn't move for a moment, as if she found the request an insult. Slender, manicured hands gripped the steering wheel. She wore an emerald-green silk tunic and linen slacks in a matching shade. The ivory skin in the V-neck of the tunic looked slightly moist and incredibly soft. There was a faint dusting of golden freckles across her nose, Ben noted idly as he took in the obvious costliness of the car and her clothing. Another bored, rich housewife, he thought cynically, up for a few days of shopping. The only thing different about this one was that she was alone. They usually came in groups, like flocks of hens. But the end result would be the same; when she went home, the back seat of the Mercedes would be packed to the roof with expensive handmade quilts, pottery, and baskets. And her old man would get the credit card charges at the end of the month.

Her lashes lifted and her glance flicked to his badge. "What did I do, Sheriff?"

Her voice was cool and controlled. It matched the rest of her, Ben thought—confident with the self-assurance conferred by wealth. They all thought the laws were made for other people.

"Your license."

For another moment Ellie stared at him. He had a rugged, weather-tanned face that just missed being handsome. From what she could see of his tall body in the khaki uniform, it was lean and athletic. His eyes were an intense blue, fringed by dark lashes, and they held a glitter of contempt that made her want to shiver.

"Oh . . . of course. I'm sorry." She fumbled in her straw bag for her billfold, found it finally and opened it to her license.

He took the billfold from her hand. Her name was Eleanor Harper and a swift calculation told him she was twenty-nine years old. The address was in Houston. His blue eyes flicked back to her face. "You're a ways from home, Mrs. Harper."

"Er . . . yes."

"Plan to be here long?"

"I don't know."

She didn't know? Was she trying to be cagey? "Well, while you're here," he said dryly, "keep in mind that this is the height of the tourist season. You'd better learn to drive defensively or you'll wreck this fine car."

His tone was edged with derision. Ellie stiffened.

He reached into his shirt pocket for a blank ticket. "Did you know you went through a red light back there?"

Automatically, Ellie glanced over her shoulder. She hadn't even seen the light. "No. I was looking for a parking place and I guess I wasn't paying attention."

"I guess," he muttered as he wrote on a small, thick pad. When he finished he ripped the top sheet off, flipped her billfold shut, and handed both billfold and ticket to her. "Around here, not paying attention will cost you twenty-five dollars," he said curtly, almost angrily.

"But I really didn't see—"

His uncompromising gaze cut her off. "This isn't Houston, Mrs. Harper," he said after a pause. "You're on my turf now, and here, ignoring red lights will get you a ticket every time."

"I didn't ignore it! I told you—" She halted when she realized that he wasn't going to listen to any excuses. A real hard-nose, this sheriff. From the way he treated traffic violators, she shuddered to think what he would do to a real criminal. "Where do I pay this?" she asked in a clipped voice.

"Clerk's office in the courthouse." He gestured with his thumb. "One street south. And you can't leave your car here. This is a no-parking zone." Before she could reply, he had turned his back and was walking to his car.

Fuming, she found the courthouse and paid the fine. She didn't mind getting the ticket so much; she *had* broken the law. It was the sheriff's manner that rankled. She hadn't ignored the light! He'd practically called her a liar.

She couldn't leave her car in the courthouse lot, but after driving around town for a half hour, she was lucky enough to find a parking space on Main Street. She'd noticed three real estate offices earlier and, after picking the most prosperous-looking one, entered Ingate's Real Estate Agency.

A robust man with a booming voice was on the telephone when she entered, and there wasn't a secretary in evidence. Ellie occupied herself by looking at color photographs of houses tacked to the walls.

She paused in front of one of the photographs, intrigued. It was a large, two-story barnlike structure with a gabled roof. The exterior was dark brown, the trim and window facings snow white. The words "Wild-horse Mill" were printed in large white block letters over the double doors.

The man finished his phone call and came around the desk, smiling, his hand extended. "Barney Ingate, ma'am."

"Hello. I'm Ellie Harper."

"What can I do for you?"

"I'm looking for a house to rent. It wouldn't have to be very large."

Ingate was shaking his head regretfully. "There hasn't been a rental house available in Springville for weeks. At the moment there aren't even any vacant apartments." He paused before adding apologetically, "I have a waiting list."

"If you put my name on your list today, what are the chances that I'd have something within a week or two?"

He shrugged. "Nil. Everything is booked up through October. There's always an outside chance that some-body will change his mind, but there are about a dozen people ahead of you."

Ellie chewed her bottom lip worriedly. All she had in the world was the money from the house in Houston, some stored furniture, and her car. She didn't want to waste her money on motel bills for very long. Turning back to the photograph tacked to the wall, she asked, "What about this?"

"That's an old-fashioned grist mill with living quar-ters on the second floor. It's for sale. Just came on the market this week. I don't know whether the owner would consider renting it or not. Anyway, it doesn't seem right for a woman. It's about nine miles out of town, and it's hard to imagine a woman operating a grist mill." His gaze scanned Ellie's slim figure in the emerald-green outfit, as if to confirm his conviction that she was the last woman he could imagine in the role.

"They grind wheat and corn—that sort of thing?" Ellie mused. "Is there really much call for that in this day and age?"

"It wouldn't be my cup of tea," Ingate said frankly. "But you'd be surprised how many people want to turn back the clock. Have their own grain ground into flour or, at least, buy it fresh ground and natural. The owner told me he'd recently started to supply several health food stores in the state. He feels there's a great potential for marketing, and he gets quite a bit of tourist trade, too."

Ellie turned back to Ingate. "Then why is he selling?"

Fleetingly she caught something in Ingate's eyes, a glint of unease, some knowledge he didn't want to reveal. "The owner is a retired minister. He bought the old mill a couple of years ago and restored it. It's nice, if you're into rustic. There's a four-room apartment on the second floor. But his wife died recently, and I guess he doesn't want to go on with it alone. Maybe it's turned into more work than he anticipated. People do impulsive things when they retire."

Or when they get a divorce? Ellie thought with sudden uncertainty. Don't make any irreversible decisions, the counselor had advised her. She shouldn't rush into buying a business before she'd even had time to get her bearings as a single woman. But, surprisingly, the idea of an old-fashioned mill fascinated her. She had a particularly warm memory of accompanying her grandfather to just such an old-fashioned mill and watching, with childish wonder, as the corn they had brought was ground into meal before her eyes. Even the smell came back as she remembered.

Why *couldn't* she try running a mill? There must be employees who knew the ropes. "Do you think the owner would lease it with an option to buy?"

Ingate's attempt to hide his surprise was not very successful. He blustered, "Well, uh—I'll present any reasonable offer."

"Could you take me out to see it now?"

That uneasy glint was back in Ingate's eyes for a moment. Then he seemed to shake off whatever it was and said, "Why, sure, Mrs. Harper. Or is it Miss?"

"Ms. will do."

"Fine. Got the key right here." He rummaged around in his desk drawer and found it. "My car's out back."

On the way to the mill he told her that there was a small guaranteed salary for the owner, since the rural area's post office was also housed in the building. After that, he kept up a one-sided conversation by describing in great detail all the improvements the owner had made at the mill.

Ask him right now what he's holding back, Ellie prodded herself, for she could still see the secretive glint that had flashed in his eyes when she'd asked why the owner was selling and again when she'd asked to see the mill. *No,* she thought, *I'll find out soon enough. It can't all be as delightfully quaint as he describes it. There must be a flaw in this somewhere.*

The photograph hadn't fully prepared her for the singular beauty of the mill house. Obviously the recipient of a recent face-lifting, the contrast between the deep brown and stark white was particularly eye-catching.

Inside, Ellie liked the sparse, utilitarian lines of the ground floor. A long counter, rescued from some turn-of-the-century post office, formed an island-divider in the center of the single, large room. It contained two narrow windows separated by a bank of open cubbyhole letter boxes.

The massive millstone, with its series of pulleys and bins for catching the grain, was at the back. On the left, a round oak table and four chairs were placed next to the wall shelves that displayed whole-wheat flour, rye flour, cornmeal, and assorted biscuit, griddle cake, and muffin mixes, all sacked in bags bearing the mill's own label—a drawing of the mill along with the words "Wildhorse Mill, Water-powered buhrstone ground, No additives or preservatives."

A plain pine staircase led to the second floor. The upstairs apartment consisted of living room, dining room, kitchen, and bath, all conveniently compact, and a large bedroom. The walls in the kitchen and dining room were paneled with ash and shone with a mellow, deep gloss of wax. The other rooms were painted a creamy beige.

The floors were of wide oak planks, also highly polished and shining like glass in the brilliant sunlight that fell through the uncurtained windows.

In that moment Ellie fell in love. The apartment looked as if it had never been lived in. It was waiting for somebody to claim it and give it a personality. She tried to picture her own modern furniture in such a setting and could not. Everything would have to be sold so that she could buy more-comfortable and homey pieces. It was the kind of furniture she would have chosen in the first place if she hadn't been married to Greg. After the ultramodern split-level house in Houston, the simplicity of the apartment would be a relief.

She turned to Ingate, her eyes shining. "This is perfect. I'd like to take a look at the books before I make an offer."

Ingate beamed. If he'd had reservations about her leasing the mill, he'd apparently dealt with them. "The owner will be here tomorrow. I'll call him then. He's only been keeping the post office open mornings since he closed the mill and moved into his cabin back in the hills. There's no telephone at the cabin, or I'd call him now."

"Tomorrow will be fine," Ellie said. "Now, Mr. Ingate, why don't you tell me what's wrong with this place."

His eyebrows rose inquiringly. "What do you mean?"

"Earlier in your office, I had a feeling that there was something about the mill you weren't telling me. I'm getting the same feeling now."

"I assure you, Ms. Harper, there is nothing wrong with the mill."

"I heard a *but* in there somewhere."

"Well . . . the hill people are a superstitious lot and . . . I might as well tell you, or somebody else will. Recently there was a tragic accident nearby. A woman drowned in Wildhorse Creek. I'm afraid it sparked some talk among the people hereabouts that the mill might be—er, well, haunted. But you don't strike me as the superstitious kind."

"You're right. I'm not." Haunted! In this day and age? "Accidents happen everywhere. The drowning has nothing to do with me, does it?"

"No—no, it doesn't," he agreed.

"I'd like to look about outside again."

She followed him down the stairs. They went out the back door and stood on the creek bank in the bright September sunlight. The huge paddle wheel sat unmoving now in the clear, swift water. Beyond the creek, a green carpet of grass, dotted thickly with trees, undulated gently over a low hill.

"It looks like a primitive painting," Ellie said, wondering what the hill people could see in such a serene setting to make them think it was haunted.

Ingate was gazing at a spot near the bottom of the wheel. Ellie, who was beginning to perspire, was puzzled to see a shiver pass through her companion. Ingate, becoming aware of her scrutiny, remarked, "Hot today, isn't it?"

She looked back at the wheel but saw nothing unusual, certainly nothing to make a grown man shiver.

She was being too sensitive. The counselor had warned her that she would be.

"Seen enough?" Ingate inquired with a note of brightness in his tone that struck her as forced.

Barney Ingate, she decided, was more affected by the superstitions surrounding this place than he would admit. This surprised her. He seemed to be such a down-to-earth person. It only proved one couldn't judge by appearances.

"For now, yes," she told him. They returned to his car. Ellie looked back over her shoulder as they drove away. The mill house surrounded by an encroaching circle of trees looked sad in the gloom of approaching dusk. Its long, white-framed windows seemed to gaze with an unblinking melancholy into the woods, as if it were lonely. The fanciful thought struck a chord in her; she felt an odd affinity with the place.

The divorce had made Ellie feel abandoned and homeless, and the mill house represented stability. It came with its own history, its own legends. If there were superstitions surrounding it, that merely gave it character. It only needed someone to shelter within its sturdy walls, someone to care for it. She pictured warm yellow light streaming from the windows, a cedar planter filled with geraniums beside the front steps, and inside, baskets of green plants hanging from the rafters.

The car followed a sharp curve in the road, and the mill house was lost from view. Ellie rested her head against the back of the seat. If the owner would consider a lease . . . No irreversible decisions, the counselor had said. She knew nothing about gristmills or living in the country. Uncharacteristically, she shoved her misgivings aside. From now on she had to make her own decisions and live with the consequences; a lease wasn't irreversible. She wanted very much to move into the mill house. She had the illogical feeling that it had been waiting just for her.

Chapter Two

*W*ithin a week Ellie had signed the papers leasing the mill house and the accompanying ten acres with an option to buy it in six months. During that week she drove out to the mill several times, and each time she fell more completely under its spell.

She had, in a manner of speaking, settled into the apartment on the second floor. After arranging to sell the furniture stored in Houston to a second-hand dealer, she'd bought the essential furnishings—a maple bed, dresser, nightstand and reading lamp of Early American design for the bedroom; a wing-back sofa covered with a provincial print and matching gold and green velvet chairs for the living room; and a small pine trestle table and two benches for the kitchen. The range was built in and the former owner had agreed to leave the refrigerator. She planned to add smaller items of furniture, curtains, and accessories slowly, when she had the time to shop for them.

Oliver Hilderbrand, a slight, solemn-faced man with an inexplicable air of disillusionment hanging over him, had spent a day with her, helping her become familiar with the mill's operation. She'd hired Jake Vining and his wife, Pearl, a tall, gaunt hill woman, to help her in the mill. They came at eight, six mornings a week, and stayed until the day's mill work was done, which usually took four or five hours.

Because the mill housed the area post office, she'd met most of her neighbors already, the closest living a half mile from the mill. The only near neighbors who hadn't been into the mill were the elderly Priscilla Gunter and Sheriff Ben Stapleton who, the Vinings told her, lived a mile north and picked up his mail in town. Remembering the sheriff's attitude upon her arrival in Springville, Ellie was glad that he wouldn't be stopping at the mill often.

She'd slept in a motel room in Springville until the night before, when the bedroom furniture had arrived, and she awoke early her first morning in the apartment feeling a deep sense of satisfaction and an almost childlike eagerness to be about the day's activities. She lay in bed for a few moments, savoring the feeling. It had been such a long time since she'd had a reason for getting up in the morning.

She showered and dressed in jeans and a yellow cotton shirt, then went downstairs to make coffee so that it would be there for Jake and Pearl when they arrived. Once the percolator was plugged in, she reached for an orange from the bowl of fruit on the oak table. It was still a little early for the Vinings, but she flipped the switch on the back wall that started the paddle wheel turning. She peeled the orange as she went outside, dropping the rinds for the birds.

Eating a juicy section of the fruit, she walked slowly around the mill house, breathing deeply of the fresh morning air and gazing at the wooded hills on all sides. Some of the leaves were beginning to turn, and the woods were losing the green verdency of summer. At the back of the mill house, she stopped on the creek bank and looked down at the rushing waters of Wild-horse Creek.

The paddle wheel made a low moaning sound as it rotated, and a small waterfall poured off each paddle as it came out of the water. This was the spot that had seemed to make Barney Ingate nervous. Although he'd been vague about where the recent drowning had occurred, Ellie suspected that it had happened here, directly behind the mill.

Continuing her walk, she saw a line of delicate yellow wild flowers growing along the edge of the woods to the north of the mill. Picturing the flowers brightening her post office counter, she finished the orange and walked toward the woods. When she bent to pick the flowers, she discovered they were entangled in a thick growth of vines. The first blossom lay in her hand separated from its stem.

As she reached for a second flower she thought she

heard a noise in the vines. She froze for a moment, listening before she straightened. It was probably nothing, but she knew there were rattlesnakes in these hills, possibly other poisonous snakes as well. It occurred to her that if she were bitten by a rattler, she could die before Jake or Pearl found her. There wasn't much hope of the neighbors hearing if she called for help. Eighty-year-old Priscilla Gunter was the closest, a half mile to the east, but everyone said she was crazy. Even if Ellie made it inside, few of the hill people had telephones.

Quite unexpectedly a scene clicked into her mind. She saw herself lying in her spartan bedroom upstairs, hands folded on her breast, with her mother, all the way from Oregon, and Greg and his new wife, Cynthia, looking down at her. Cynthia was wearing one of those high-fashion originals that she favored.

Ellie smiled at the thought. What made her imagine that Cynthia would bother to come to her funeral? Probably Greg wouldn't come either. He'd just send flowers with a small white card written in his flowing script: "For the good memories, Greg," or something equally as phony. He might even shed a tear or two for her. People often seemed more attractive after they were gone.

Suddenly Ellie was laughing, her head thrown back. The laughter gurgled from her until tears ran down her cheeks. She wiped the tears with the tail of her shirt. It was probably a reaction to the tension she'd been under lately, but it felt pretty good to laugh. She couldn't remember when she'd laughed that hard. She enjoyed poking fun at herself sometimes, but Mrs. Greg Harper had forgotten how to laugh. Dear heaven, what had Greg done to her, what had she let him do?

At twenty, she'd thought that her ready laughter was one of the things that had attracted Greg to her when he was a poor medical student and she a legal secretary. But after they were married, he'd immediately started trying to change her. She must be more sophisticated, more serious, as befitted the wife of an up-and-coming plastic surgeon. Greg had tried to mold her inside as he redesigned his patients' outsides. And she had worked hard at being malleable. A futile exercise, as it turned out, for Greg had found the beautiful Cynthia, twelve years his junior, and apparently exactly what Greg wanted, outside and in, without any troublesome revamping.

When Ellie learned about Cynthia, she thought her life had ended. *She* was Mrs. Greg Harper. If Greg left her, who would she be? She had looked around in a panic for someone to confide in and had discovered that she had a lot of acquaintances, but no real friends. It was a new and frightening perspective from which to view her life.

Eventually she'd been able to admit to herself that she didn't feel comfortable in the elaborate, sprawling, modern house that Greg had bought for them, without consulting her. She realized that she didn't particularly like the people they saw socially—that, in fact, she heartily disliked quite a few of them. She found out that she'd been married for nine years to a man with whom she had little in common and whom, as far as any deep level of empathy or understanding went, she hardly knew.

All of these insights were new to her, and they rocked her to her core. Until very recently she'd never really pulled back from her role as Greg's wife and taken a good hard look at herself. The counselor had helped her do that, and now she realized that she'd been unhappy for some time but had refused to think about it. She had become expert at not thinking about anything that distressed her. What had terrified her the most was that she seemed to have so little inner strength to draw on in a crisis. She'd left Houston determined to find that strength, to find herself.

Ellie forced her mind away from Greg and the past. He had never really loved her, she thought now, and her love for him had died long ago. But she had learned a vital lesson from him: She had to make her own life. It was foolish to depend too much on another person.

Birds sang in the woods, and over the slap and grind of the wheel the drone of a tractor came to her from a farm to the east. She carefully picked a handful of the yellow wild flowers, avoiding the vines, and carried them inside. She put the flowers in a brown ironstone vase and set them on the post office counter where customers would see them when they entered.

As she finished, she heard the mail truck pulling into the drive. Behind the truck, the Vinings' ancient rattle-trap Dodge pickup could be heard. Pearl would be driving. She always drove because Jake's eyesight was failing.

The mail carrier, a fresh-faced young man named

Dennis, got out of the truck with a bundle of mail in one arm, a Styrofoam cup in his hand. "Morning, Ellie." They had settled on first names the day before. "Got any coffee on?"

Ellie grinned at him. "A full pot." She filled Dennis's cup along with three mugs that she took from pegs on the wall. Dennis left as Jake and Pearl came in.

Jake took his coffee back to the grain bins, saying, "Better get started on that corn." Pearl sat down at the table with Ellie.

Sandy freckles covered Pearl's thin, pale face, and a deep dimple high on one cheek, which was visible even when Pearl wasn't smiling, seemed strangely out of place. Pearl's brassy red hair was pulled to the back of her head and wound into a large knot. The hair had never been cut, Pearl had informed Ellie, because her religion forbade it. Ellie had discovered that, in spite of Pearl's unusual religious beliefs, she was a warm, good-natured woman.

"I'd better start sacking the meal," Pearl said.

"Finish your coffee first."

"I noticed yesterday that we're short on the griddle cake mix. I'll make up some of that and sack it after I finish with the meal."

Ellie nodded absently. "Last night I looked through the orders that have accumulated over the past few weeks. I'll need to make some arrangements for deliveries. I'd like to do it myself the first time or two. I think I ought to get to know my customers."

"Mr. Hilderbrand made his own deliveries. That's why he bought that van of his."

"Do you think he'd rent me the van for a day now and then?"

Pearl reflected for a moment. "Can't think why not. He worked hard getting those customers. He wouldn't want the mill to lose them. He had big plans to expand the business across the state line."

"He mentioned that to me. You know, Pearl, it's so obvious that he loves this place. I keep wondering why he leased it."

"Seems like he just lost heart when Mandy died," Pearl said. "He didn't want to be around people so much."

"When did Mrs. Hilderbrand die?"

"Not long ago," Pearl said vaguely.

"Maybe it wasn't a good idea for him to put it on the market so quickly. He might come to regret it."

"That's what I thought," Pearl admitted. "But 'twern't none of my business."

Ellie was remembering Barney Ingate's inexplicable behavior on the afternoon he'd brought her out to the mill, especially when they had been standing on the creek bank behind the mill house. "Pearl, how did Mandy Hilderbrand die?"

Pearl shifted uneasily in her chair and lifted the coffee mug to her lips. After a moment, she said, "It was an accident, Ellie."

"Did she drown?"

Pearl hesitated.

"It happened here, didn't it?" Ellie persisted. "Out back, behind the mill house."

Pearl's hazel eyes looked troubled. Finally she said,

"She fell into the creek. It was bad enough that she drowned, but her head got caught under the mill wheel and when—"

"Pearl!" Jake bawled. "This bin is about to overflow. Quit your gabbin' and come help me sack."

Pearl got up abruptly and went to her husband. It seemed to Ellie that the other woman was relieved. Pearl, ordinarily garrulous, hadn't wanted to talk about Mandy Hilderbrand's death. Although warm sunlight fell through a front window onto the table where she sat, briefly Ellie felt a chill. She could understand Pearl's reluctance. Losing his wife in such a way must have been a dreadful shock to Oliver Hilderbrand. No wonder he seemed so sad.

Ellie went behind the post office counter to sort the bundle Dennis had left. About a half hour later, area residents began coming in to pick up their mail and buy postage or mill products. When Oliver Hilderbrand appeared, Ellie asked him if he'd be willing to rent her his van. He seemed willing enough, agreeing to leave the van at the mill house the next Wednesday and pick it up when Ellie returned from her first round of deliveries. Ellie offered to let him drive her car while she had the van, but he declined, saying he would enjoy the long walk to his cabin back in the hills.

Shortly after noon, a young woman Ellie hadn't seen before came into the mill. She was a few years older than Ellie, with shining black hair tied back with a pink satin ribbon, and great gray eyes that sparkled with a zest for life. Even the jeans and loose cotton shirt she wore could not hide the voluptuous lines of her figure. She was lovely.

Ellie was stacking sacks of cornmeal and griddle cake mix on the shelves along one wall when the woman entered, looked around, saw Ellie, and smiled warmly. "You must be Ellie Harper." She came forward, hand extended. "I'm Liz Pembrook."

The woman's grip on Ellie's hand was firm and businesslike. "I've been wanting to meet you," Liz went on. "Barney Ingate told me a woman had leased the mill, but somehow I pictured you as older."

Ellie laughed. "I'm feeling older. I'm sore from all the bending and stretching I've been doing, but I'll get used to it."

Liz peered around the post office divider to the back of the room and waved. "Hi, Pearl, Jake."

Pearl left the meal bin to come toward Liz and Ellie.

"Did you finish those quilts?" Liz asked Pearl.

"Just did," Pearl told her. "I left the back door open for you. They're on the kitchen table."

"Good. I think I've already sold both of them." Liz turned to Ellie. "I own a craft shop in Springville. Pearl's handmade quilts are in great demand."

"I didn't know you were so talented, Pearl," Ellie said.

Pearl threw up her bony hands, which were covered with meal dust. "Pshaw! I been piecing quilts since I was a child. Till Liz here talked me into letting her sell some of them, I never thought of it as a talent. When I was growing up, it was a necessity." Pearl's chin lifted proudly. "I will say that my mother was the neatest stitcher in these hills. She taught me all her secrets."

"I must see those quilts," Ellie told Liz eagerly. "I

haven't finished furnishing my apartment, and I'd like to use some of the local crafts."

Liz's gray eyes danced. "We're in the middle of a big boom in native crafts here. Tourists can't get enough of them. When I opened my shop four years ago and went out in search of craftspeople, I was amazed at the talent hidden in these hills. I have every kind of needlework you can imagine, handmade brooms and baskets, handwoven rugs and cloth, and some beautiful pottery." She laughed. "Don't get me started! But you must come to my shop. It's Ozark Crafts, and it's on Main Street. If you want to see Pearl's quilts, though, you'd better make it in the next day or two. I promised to hold them for a woman in Fayetteville, and she'll be here at the end of the week."

"I was going to town tomorrow, anyway," Ellie said. "I'll come by."

"I'll get back to my sacking," Pearl said. "We're about finished for today." She returned to the bin where she had been working when Liz came in.

"Gotta run," Liz said. "I have several more stops to make before going back to town."

Ellie liked this vivacious woman. "Can't you stay long enough for a cup of coffee?"

"Okay," Liz agreed. "I always have time for coffee."

Ellie filled two mugs and the two women sat at the oak table.

"You're lucky to have the Vinings working for you," Liz said.

"Ummm," Ellie agreed. "I hope they're going to stay for a long time. Jake talks about retiring." She lowered her voice and leaned toward Liz. "He doesn't see very well, but he doesn't like to admit it. Not that he needs to see well. He's been doing mill work for so long I think he could do it blindfolded. When he said he wasn't up to working nine or ten hours a day any more, I asked if he knew someone who could help him. He brought Pearl, and they usually manage to finish by noon or shortly after. It's worked out well for me, having the two of them here. I came into this business green."

"Where are you fron?"

"I've been living in Houston, but my grandparents lived and died in the Ozarks, about fifty miles from here. I used to spend summers with them, and I fell in love with this country. So when the big city got to be too much . . ."

Liz's head was tilted to one side. She was listening to Ellie's recital with keen interest. Ellie smiled faintly. "I was recently divorced. Maybe I'm trying to kick over the traces." She glanced about the large room. "This is about as far removed from my life in Houston as I could get."

"Sometimes it's the only way. Scrap everything and start over someplace else."

Ellie nodded. "Being on my own is new to me; so is running a grist mill. I'm just bumbling along as if I knew what I was doing."

"Living alone has its advantages." Liz chuckled. "I should know. I've never married."

"Not for lack of opportunities, I'll bet."

Liz shrugged. "I'm too stubborn and self-willed for

most men. Anyway, the shop takes most of my time. I'm certainly not bored! All in all, I'm pretty contented with my life." Liz finished her coffee. "I'll see you tomorrow at the shop." She grinned mischievously. "Bring your checkbook. You'll find you can't resist some of my crafts." She called good-bye to Jake and Pearl and hurried out the door.

Ellie wandered back to where the Vinings were emptying the last bin of cornmeal.

"Good-lookin' woman, that Liz Pembrook," Jake observed.

Pearl snorted. "How'd you know?"

"I ain't that blind!" Jake said with a sly grin.

Ellie said, "I'd like to get to know her better. She's so alive, so sure of herself."

Pearl looked thoughtful. "Folks around here thought she'd marry the sheriff before now. They stepped out together regular for years. They was high school sweethearts. Then all of a sudden, last year, it was off. I always thought it was because Liz couldn't give up that all-fired independence she's so high on."

Jake pulled a small paper sack from his overalls pocket, opened it, and tore off a plug of tobacco. "Maybe it was Ben who couldn't give up his independence. He didn't act too broke up when he and Liz called it quits." He tucked the tobacco into his cheek.

"He puts up a good front," Pearl conceded. "Ben ain't the kind of man to wear his heart on his sleeve."

Jake grunted around the plug of tobacco. "Reckon he'll live," he remarked sarcastically.

Pearl was wiping her hands clean on a towel that

hung on a rack near the grain bins. "You men," she said complacently, "always stick together."

Ellie was trying to picture Liz and Ben Stapleton together. Outwardly, they seemed a perfect match, two intelligent, good-looking people. What had really happened between them? Her curiosity about that surprised her, and she chided herself for it. Maybe Liz didn't relish living with such a grouch. And who knew what went on in Ben Stapleton's head?

Jake pulled down on the switch, stopping the paddle wheel, then got the broom and dustpan and began to sweep the board floor around the grain bins. Hearing one of the large double doors open, Ellie and Pearl walked toward the front. A teenage boy had stepped inside. Ellie judged him to be about seventeen, but he was small for his age—skinny, with greasy brown hair and a scattering of acne on his forehead and cheeks.

"Hi, Jimmy," Pearl greeted him. "How's your old granny?"

The boy shot a quick, furtive look at Ellie, then blushed. "About the same." He stepped to one of the letterboxes and took out the envelope resting there. "Here's Gran's pension check. She's been looking for it for two weeks. She loses track of time." He turned toward Ellie but seemed to be too shy to meet her gaze. "Miss Harper, Gran wanted me to get a sack of cornmeal and see if you would put it on our bill."

Ellie knew this had to be Jimmy Gunter, grandson of her nearest neighbor, "crazy" Priscilla Gunter. She also knew that Oliver Hilderbrand had allowed them to run up small bills and pay whenever they were able.

"Sure, Jimmy." She got a sack of meal from the shelf and handed it to him. "Bring your grandmother in sometime. I want to meet all my neighbors."

· Jimmy took the sack and ducked his head. "Gran don't get around much, ma'am."

When he was gone, Pearl said, "Priscilla gets out more than Jimmy lets on. She wanders in the woods at night sometimes. Right spooky when you think about it." She made a clucking sound. "I'd be careful about letting that boy have too much credit. Old Priscilla likely won't remember to pay you, and that Jimmy might not be around here too much longer. He and two other boys broke into the high school and stole some stuff. Some of it the police never found. There's goin' to be a court trial over it. He could get a jail term."

"What a shame," Ellie said sadly. "What will his grandmother do without him?"

Pearl shook her head. "She'll make out, I reckon. They say God looks out for those that can't look out for themselves."

"Wouldn't Mrs. Gunter be better off in a nursing home?"

Pearl grunted. "They'd have to hog-tie her to get her to leave here, and they'd have to keep her tied up or she'd run away and come back."

"How long has she been . . . ?"

"Crazy, you mean? Must be nearly three years now. I saw her the day before it happened, and she was just as clear-headed as you or me."

Ellie looked at Pearl, puzzled at her words. She had assumed that Priscilla Gunter was senile, but senility came on gradually, not overnight. "I don't understand. The day before what happened?"

"The day before she saw that haint."

Ellie stared, uncomprehending for a moment. "Haint?" she repeated, vaguely recalling her own grandmother having used that word. "You mean ghost?"

"Haint, ghost, spirit, whatever you want to call it. That's what made Priscilla Gunter lose her mind."

It was clear that Pearl believed what she was saying. Ellie hardly knew how to respond. "Wh-what happened?"

"Well, it was the dead of winter, and Priscilla had walked to a box supper down at the Mountain View Church. On the way home, all of a sudden, she saw a little child with blond curls all over his head, walking beside her. There was a family that lived about a mile and a half from the church on that old road, and Priscilla thought it was their little boy, but she did think it was strange, them lettin' that child wander around on a winter night like that.

"Well, she tried to pick up the child 'cause it was whimpering and only wearing a thin nightgown. But every time she tried to get hold of him, he'd move away. Then she noticed the poor little tyke was barefooted, and that child walked right at her heels every step up that mountain."

Ellie was fascinated in spite of herself. Pearl continued, "Priscilla decided those people must have left the child in the church by accident, and she thought she'd just turn off at their lane so he'd follow her. When she came to a little stream—just a trickle, really, narrow enough to step across—why, the child fell down and spread out his little arms and disappeared. A ghost won't cross water, you know. That's when Priscilla realized the thing that had been walking beside her wasn't no human child. She took off running and ran all the way home, but she ain't never been the same since. She started to act queer right after that. Of course, that story got around and everybody thought it was little William Swafford that Priscilla had seen. He was Mandy Hilderbrand's baby brother who got lost and et up by coyotes or some other wild beasts."

Ellie was so engrossed in what Pearl was saying that she hadn't heard Jake come up behind her. When he spoke, she jumped.

"Don't pay Pearl no mind, Ellie," the old man said. "She does love to tell ghost stories. She don't believe half she tells, though."

"Humph!" Pearl retorted. "I believe what Priscilla said happened to her really did happen, and so do you, Jake Vining. We saw her the next day when she was half out of her mind."

"Are you telling me there was nothing wrong with Priscilla Gunter's mind before that, and afterward she was insane?" Ellie asked incredulously.

"She ain't all that insane," Jake muttered crossly. "She has days when she's clear-headed. But then there's days when she's mixed up." He turned to his wife. "Let's go. We still got chores to do at home."

As soon as they had shut the door behind them, Ellie released a sound of amazement. Pearl Vining actually believed what she had said. And in spite of Jake's protestations, Ellie thought he more than half believed it himself. She could imagine the condescension with which her sophisticated crowd in Houston would react to the Vinings. Not so long ago she would have reacted similarly, as she'd been programmed. Not that she was now willing to consider the possibility that ghosts existed. But she was willing to treat Pearl and Jake and their opinions with respect.

This thought pleased her. Maybe Greg hadn't completely obliterated the old Ellie after all.

Chapter Three

As usual, a small rush of customers arrived between four and closing time at five. And still the trickle of tourists continued and would go on, everyone told her, until winter set in. Desire to see an operating gristmill drew them the nine miles out of Springville; owners of shops such as Liz Pembrook's were happy to spread the word about the mill to their customers. It was not uncommon for a tourist to buy two or three grocery sacks full of the mill's flour, meal, and dry mixes—a supply for themselves and more for relatives and friends. Ellie also did a brisk business in honey, sorghum, pecans, and walnuts, which she bought from farmers in the area.

Added to the postmistress's salary, it began to look

as if the mill profits would provide her with an adequate income, even allowing for the slowdown of business during the winter.

After closing, she decided to sample some of her own wares. In the small kitchen upstairs, she made dough for whole-wheat bread, "kneading away her wearies," as her grandmother used to say, and set it in loaf pans to rise. After a late supper, she wrote a letter to her mother—who had married a widower four years previously and lived in Oregon—all the while keeping an eye on the bread as it baked and filled the apartment with its rich, yeasty aroma.

She went to bed after the late television news and slept immediately. It was much later when she awoke abruptly, as if she'd been startled out of a bad dream. But if she had been dreaming, she couldn't remember it. She sat up in bed in the heavy darkness of the bedroom, wondering what had disturbed her sleep. She fumbled for the bedside clock, turning its luminous face so that she could read it. Ten after one.

Then she heard the noise that must have awakened her. A scraping sound, as if metal moved against a rough surface. The noise continued for several moments, stopped, and started again. It seemed to come from below. She switched on the bedside lamp and reached for her robe which lay across the foot of the bed.

But in the living room, she just stood and looked at the locked apartment door, her heart pounding. She couldn't make herself open it and go down to investigate. Then she heard the noise again and fright gripped her. Someone was down there trying to get in! She looked around in a panic for something to use as a weapon. Her gaze fell on the telephone. But who could she call? The Vinings had no phone. Then she remembered that the sheriff lived only a mile away.

Her hands shook as she leafed through the phone book until she found his number. She hesitated only a moment longer. Ben Stapleton wasn't the person she would have called for help if she'd had a choice, but he was her only close neighbor with a phone. And he *was* the sheriff. He was getting paid to protect people.

He finally answered on the fifth ring. His voice was slurred by sleep. "Sheriff Stapleton speaking."

Ellie's fingers tightened on the receiver. "This is Eleanor Harper, Sheriff. I bought the Hilderbrand mill."

A moment's silence followed. Then, "I heard."

His tone sounded so flat and disinterested that Ellie was very tempted to hang up on him. But there wasn't anyone else she could call. While she tried to decide how to state her problem, silence hummed between them.

The sheriff drew a put-upon breath and grated, "I presume you had a reason for calling me in the middle of the night, Ms. Harper."

There was no sound from below now. Ellie said in a small voice, "I think somebody was trying to break into the mill."

"Did you see someone?" At least he sounded more alert.

"No, it was a scraping noise from downstairs, as though somebody was trying to pick a lock."

"You haven't gone downstairs?"

"No. I don't have a weapon." She tried to sound merely prudent, but the fact was she was to terrified to go downstairs alone. But she wasn't going to admit it to Ben Stapleton.

"Okay, stay where you are. I'll come over and check it out." He hung up before she could reply. He made her feel like a fool.

Without the connection to another human voice, the silence pressed in on her. Her isolation in the mill house, which she had welcomed before, now seemed almost threatening. Determinedly, she shook off the feeling. *You are not helpless, Ellie.* She straightened her shoulders and, going to the kitchen closet, took out the broom. It wasn't much of a weapon, but it was better than nothing. Gripping the handle, she moved silently to the living room door and turned the lock. Opening the door carefully, she strained to hear. Stillness enveloped her. Reassured, she stepped onto the second floor landing and flipped the switch that turned on the downstairs lights.

She stood on the landing for long minutes, clutching the broom and listening. Nothing. She took a deep breath and began slowly to descend the stairs. Halfway down she could bend over and see most of the ground floor. Everything looked just as she had left it—the post office counter, bare except for the postal scales and the vase of yellow wild flowers. At the back, the empty bins and idle pulley and millstone waited for the sunrise and the day's work to begin.

At that moment, she heard the scraping sound again. She started, ready to retreat to the second floor if need be. She stared at the front door, but it didn't move. When the sound came again, she realized that it wasn't coming from the front of the mill house. It seemed to come from the north side of the room between the grain bins and the shelves filled with flour and meal.

She didn't know how many minutes she stood there, unmoving, waiting for the sound to come again before a sharp knock sounded at the door.

"Ms. Harper, open up! It's the sheriff."

Limp with relief, Ellie flew down the remainder of the stairs and opened the door. Ben Stapleton, wearing jeans and a cream-colored Windbreaker, looked down at her, standing there in her robe still clutching the broom. He seemed more intrigued than annoyed as she propped the broom against the wall.

"Come in," she said breathlessly. "I heard that noise again a few minutes ago. It seemed to be coming from over there."

"What's the broom for?" he inquired laconically as he crossed the room at her heels.

She turned to look up at him. He noted the high color in her face and the receding fright in her dark eyes. Her auburn hair was mussed from the bed, and the white satin robe she wore revealed small, firm breasts, a narrow waist, and intriguingly rounded hips beneath its glimmering fabric. Ben was fascinated. She was an eyeful, all right, especially as she looked now, ready for bed. And scared of her own shadow, it appeared. Liz had told him that Eleanor Harper had been recently divorced, and Ben was unexpectedly curious about that. What was the story behind the breakup of her marriage? And why in creation did she want to move out here in the country alone? Maybe she was a flake.

"I was going to use it to defend myself if I had to," she said, lifting her chin as though daring him to make something of it. The action exposed the smooth ivory line of her throat to Ben's interested scrutiny.

"Ms. Harper," he drawled, "if you're going to attack an intruder, you'd better be damn sure you can knock him cold or you'll be in worse trouble than before."

"You don't think anybody was here, do you?"

"I don't know," he replied frankly.

"You think I imagined it." She put her hands on her hips and cocked her head to one side. The white satin stretched over her breasts.

"Maybe," he said easily. "I checked outside before I came in. There's nobody around now."

"I heard something." Her voice was raised in indignation.

His blue eyes swept over her. "If sounds in the night scare you, Ms. Harper, you shouldn't be living out here. This is no place for a woman like you."

"What do you mean, a woman like me?"

He thrust his hands into the pockets of his Windbreaker and there was a lift of his brow. "Obviously you're used to city living. A nice house in a nice secure neighborhood. The beauty parlor on Tuesdays and bridge at the country club on Thursdays."

Ellie made a low sound of anger. The fact that his scornful remark had come very close to describing her life in Houston did nothing to lessen her fury. "Do you always make snap judgments without evidence, Sheriff?"

He laughed then. "You're the evidence, lady. The way you act, the way you dress." His gaze fell to her robe for a moment and then, as if he had lost interest, he sauntered over to the wall next to the grain bins. "You say the sound came from over here?"

Ellie followed him slowly, thrown off balance by the sudden change in subject. "Yes, down there near the floor."

He glanced over his shoulder and watched her tug the tie belt of her robe more tightly. "Perfectly simple explanation. Don't they have mice in Houston, Ms. Harper?"

"Mice!"

He shrugged. "Or maybe it was a rat. Whatever, it must have been between the foundation walls trying to get out."

Ellie's cheeks burned with embarrassment. He was right, damn him. The explanation *was* simple, and it hadn't even occurred to her. She felt like a complete idiot.

She walked away from him. "I'm not used to living alone, and I guess I overreacted. I apologize for getting you over here for nothing."

"This isn't the first time I've gotten out of bed to go on a wild goose chase." He ambled to the door and halted to look at the broom propped against the wall. "If I were you, I'd get a bat."

Ellie glared at him. "Thank you for the advice, Sheriff."

He grinned as he opened the door and stepped outside. She had an almost irresistible urge to hurl something at his back. She slammed the door shut and turned the lock.

Ben climbed into his car and started the engine. He was humming a tune under his breath as he drove away. He ought to be furious about having his sleep interrupted by a hysterical woman afraid of a mouse. But damn if he hadn't enjoyed explaining the obvious to her. She'd looked delectable in that satin robe, if preposterously out of place. She had about as much business running a gristmill as he'd have embroidering doilies. She baffled him.

So, he thought as he steered the car slowly along the deserted gravel road toward home. She's an attractive woman with an air of mystery about her. That doesn't mean she isn't a neurotic, brainless piece of fluff going through some kind of back-to-nature phase. Maybe her ex-husband had had good reason to divorce her.

Ellie turned out the lights and went back upstairs, trying not to think about the ninny she'd made of herself in front of Ben Stapleton. Tomorrow she would have to check for cracks where mice might enter. The grain would be a magnet to rodents, so she would have to make certain they couldn't get in.

Back in her bed, she looked into the darkness, finding it difficult to banish the sheriff's stalwart face from her memory. Why hadn't she investigated before phoning him? She could hardly blame him for thinking her a flighty woman with a big imagination. But she did blame him, damn it!

Sighing, she turned on her side. Silver moonlight made its way through the window beside her bed and lay on the oak floorboards, gentle and warm as an embrace. For a fleeting second a niggle of fear tried to push its way into her consciousness, a hint of menace that did not belong with the serenity of the night and the peaceful rural setting. Ellie, she told herself, you've got to get a grip on yourself. Face it, as much as you'd like to deny it, you were affected by Pearl's ghost story and learning how Mandy Hilderbrand died. You actually let it work on your imagination until you felt a presence in the mill house. Then when you heard that mouse, you jumped to the most farfetched conclusion instead of the obvious one.

She fell asleep finally and didn't wake again until after seven. Hazy sunlight was falling through the bedroom window and, when she looked out, she saw the sun was obscured by a gray cloud cover. She hurried to dress, eat breakfast, and have the coffee made downstairs before eight o'clock.

"I'll be making deliveries Friday," she told Jake when he and Pearl arrived, "so I'll need some more rye and whole-wheat flour. Pearl, if you have time, I'd like to take along samples of the mixes, too. I don't understand why Mr. Hilderbrand didn't have more orders for them."

"They're new," Pearl told her. "The mixes were my idea. I was in here waiting for Jake to finish work one day and the thought came to me that some quick mixes made from natural ingredients ought to sell."

"I'll bet they're your recipes, too," Ellie said.

Pearl grinned. "You're right. You can't expect a man to know about things like that, and Mandy wasn't much of a cook, either. But Jake and Mr. Hilderbrand only made up the first batch of mixes about a week before Mandy died. I wrote down all the recipes on cards and put them in the back of the stamp drawer."

"I'll take along as much as we can get made up then," Ellie decided. "I have a feeling they'll sell like"—she laughed—"like griddle cakes."

A long table placed next to the staircase wall made a good work area for putting together the mixes. In between customers, Ellie helped Pearl sack them all morning.

"I'll check into freight charges for shipping the orders after I meet the customers personally. If the business grows, as I hope it will, I won't be able to keep making deliveries myself."

"You could end up spending all your time on the road," Pearl agreed, "and you'd have to buy your own van, too."

"Which would defeat my purpose in moving to the country for peace and quiet, wouldn't it?"

Pearl dumped another sack of freshly ground flour into the large pot she was using for mixing. "Lots of women wouldn't want to stay out here alone," she said judiciously.

Ellie darted a sharp glance at Pearl. She couldn't have heard about Ellie's call to the sheriff already. "I had a few second thoughts last night," Ellie said finally. "I woke up about one and heard a noise down here." She didn't want to admit that she'd rousted Ben

Stapleton out of bed. She added lightly, "I thought at first it might be that ghost of yours."

Pearl frowned at her. "I expect it was just your imagination."

Was her emotional state so obvious? "Actually I think it was a mouse."

Pearl's grave expression didn't alter. "My pa always said when a haint comes back, it's most usually because it was murdered and wants the murderer brought to justice. When my pa was a boy, he had an aunt that was smothered to death by her husband. Leastwise, that's what Pa believed. Only everybody thought she died of heart failure. She used to run a loom in an old loom house built behind the family home. After she died, her husband tore down the loom house and went courtin' another woman. Married her two months after his first wife died. After he brought his bride home, they kept hearing the boards a-rattlin' out back just like the old loom was runnin'. They heard that loom rattlin' every night. Then one night my aunt's ghost walked right up to the door."

Pearl laughed shortly. "That new wife packed up and the both of 'em moved out of there fast! Moved clear out of the county. They never did bring that man to justice, but my family always believed he killed Pa's aunt. I've often wondered if that poor ghost ever managed to rest in peace."

"Ghost!" Pearl's voice had risen at the end of her story and Jake had heard her. "Pearl, will you stop goin' on about ghosts! You know you don't believe that stuff."

"Lots of smart people have believed in spirits," Pearl retorted. "Ellie heard something last night and I was explaining that ghosts don't come back unless they've been murdered or suffered some other terrible wrong they want righted. I was trying to reassure her—"

"Reassure her! It was probably that crazy tale you told yesterday that made her hear things in the first place. What are you trying to do? This gal is here at night by herself."

"Pearl's ghost stories don't bother me, Jake," Ellie said. She wouldn't let them! She was a sensible, mature woman, for heaven's sake. "It was only a mouse last night. Which reminds me. Shouldn't we check for cracks where they might get inside?"

"I did that for Mr. Hilderbrand already. Used up three boxes of steel wool, but I stuffed up every crack I could find. Don't you worry, Ellie, there ain't no mouse gonna get in here."

Ellie wasn't thoroughly convinced. With Jake's poor eyesight, he could have missed something. Later, she'd check for cracks herself.

"Say," Pearl said, "weren't you supposed to go to town this morning?"

"We've been so busy, I forgot," Ellie exclaimed. "Oh, well, it's too late now. I can put it off another day, I guess."

"No need for that," Jake said. "I'll stay and take care of things here till you get back. Pearl can go home and do the chores and come back for me later."

"Are you sure you wouldn't mind?"

"Not a bit," Jake assured her.

Ellie ran upstairs to change clothes, wondering again how she would manage without the Vinings. They were so much help to her, she could surely reciprocate by listening to Pearl's ghost stories now and then. *Think of it as local color, Ellie.*

Liz Pembrook's shop was tucked into a corner of Main Street. The bell attached to the door jingled as Ellie entered. No one was in sight, but Ellie saw an open door at the back leading into another room. She walked to a display counter and examined some attractive pottery. She picked up a mug and turned it over in her hand. The exterior was a soft chocolate brown with a gentle robin's-egg blue inside. Single place settings of several pottery designs were displayed. Ellie was especially taken with a soft brown teapot with handpainted yellow wild flowers on it, like the flowers she had picked from her own yard.

Noticing that no prices were in evidence, she smiled. This was no place to buy cheap Ozark souvenirs. Liz Pembrook's merchandise was top quality and no price tags usually meant "expensive."

"I thought I heard the bell." Liz, wearing a softly tailored blue cotton dress, came toward her from the back room. "Why didn't you yell?"

"I was too busy looking. You have some really gorgeous things. I don't see Pearl's quilts, though."

"The needlework's in the other room. Come with me."

The second room was almost as large as the first, and its shelves and display counters were filled with needlepoint pillows, crewel embroidered scenes framed for hanging, crocheted and knitted afghans, hand-braided rugs, bolts of hand-woven cloth, and quilts.

Liz spread a quilt across one of the counters. It had a pale blue background with sprays of appliquéd irises, in darker blue and lavender scattered across it. "This is one of Pearl's," Liz said. "Look at the stitching. It's so uniform you'd swear it was done by machine."

Ellie ran a hand over the padded surface. The intricate quilting design was indeed meticulously done. "It's lovely! Wouldn't it make a pretty coverlet over a blue dust ruffle?"

Liz chuckled. "Stop drooling. This one's sold."

"It's the wrong color, anyway. My bedroom walls are beige."

"Pearl does a sunflower pattern that would be perfect. Why don't you talk to her about it? You could deal directly with her and save my commission. Pearl works exclusively for me, but since you're her other employer, I think we could make an exception. Don't tell anybody, though."

"I won't."

"While we're on the subject of your bedroom . . ." Liz went on, "come look at this piece of fabric." She went to a shelf against one wall and lifted down a bolt of loosely woven hand-loomed material striped in browns, yellows, and greens. "Imagine draperies made from this."

"Stop tempting me," Ellie laughed. "I've only leased the mill house. I'd better wait until I'm sure I'm staying before I spend too much on it. But I do want that teapot in the other room."

While Liz packaged the teapot, she said, "I hope you stay here, Ellie. I'd like us to be friends."

"So would I."

Liz handed her the package. "Let's walk across the street to the café and have something to drink."

Ellie agreed and Liz locked the door, hanging a "Back in fifteen minutes" sign against the glass.

In the small café, they took a table near the back and ordered soft drinks. As they waited, Ellie glanced toward the front and saw a tall, dark-haired man in a khaki law officer's uniform enter. Ben Stapleton. Oh, God, she hoped he didn't see them.

Before he had a chance to, Liz saw him and, to Ellie's dismay, called to him, "Ben! Join us."

Ellie watched him angling his way around the tables and coming toward them. For an instant, she rested her forehead on the heel of her hand. All too clearly, she could picture herself opening the door to Ben last night, wearing her satin robe and carrying that stupid broom. With perfect clarity, she heard herself explaining that somebody had tried to break into the mill house.

She hated making a fool of herself, hated more doing it in front of Ben Stapleton. From their first meeting, Ellie had recognized a man who did not suffer fools gladly. Worse than that, there was some perverse streak in her that found the sheriff attractive. In spite of his unwelcoming attitude toward her, she had to admit it. He had a strength of character. He was a simple man at ease with himself, "real." So different from Greg and the other men she had known in Houston. Her battered self-esteem was attracted to that.

Drawing around herself the aloof facade that she had learned to hide behind while married to Greg, she lifted her head and met Ben's clear, blue gaze.

Chapter Four

$\mathcal{H}$e turned to the waitress and asked for coffee as he sat down at their table.

"Ellie, this is our county sheriff, Ben Stapleton."

Ellie thought she detected laughter in the sheriff's eyes. "We've met."

Ben took in her dark eyes, which were cool and steady, but her cheeks turned as pink as the lacy blouse she wore. She was really galled about having made such a stir over a mouse and blaming him because he'd witnessed her embarrassment. Ben eyed her with a small smile. She was actually blushing. Once in a while she let that big city veneer slip a little. It made Ben wonder about the woman behind the facade. When he'd stopped her for running the red light and again last night, he'd detected a quick flare of temper in her, immediately banked. Maybe his first assessment of her hadn't been totally correct. These small signs of warmth and passion teased his curiosity.

"Ellie is running the old Swafford mill," Liz was saying.

Ben grinned, and Ellie found herself thinking that she wasn't surprised that Liz might have considered marrying him. Had she broken Ben's heart, as Pearl thought? Realizing that she was staring at Ben's mouth, Ellie shifted her gaze and reached for her soda as the waitress set it down.

"I know," Ben drawled. "We're neighbors."

"That's right, I forgot," Liz said. "I'm glad the mill's open again. Tourists love it. Ellie, you've managed to confuse Barney Ingate. He was convinced you would back out on your agreement to lease the mill, right up until you moved in. You just aren't Barney's idea of a mill manager."

"I don't seem to be a lot of people's idea of a mill manager," Ellie said, looking at Ben challengingly. "Why is that, Sheriff?"

"I guess," Ben responded, "people think a woman who would want to live out there and run a mill must be either a recluse or a tough cookie." He gazed at her appraisingly. "You don't seem to be a recluse, so you must be a tough cookie, appearances to the contrary."

Somehow she knew he was thinking about her quaking over hearing a mouse in the middle of the night. The man was laughing at her! He had a positive knack for infuriating her. The three times she had seen him, he'd made her want to throw things. She couldn't remember being so touchy since her teenage years.

This must be the kind of overreaction the counselor had warned her about.

"I'll learn to be as tough as I have to be, Sheriff."

"What is it with you men?" Liz challenged. "Do you think an independent woman has to look like a lady wrestler?"

Ben shrugged good-naturedly. "By a lucky coincidence, I seem to have found the two exceptions to the rule. How are the plans for the class reunion coming, Liz?"

"Our high school class is having its fifteenth reunion in a couple of weeks," Liz explained to Ellie. To Ben she said, "Reservations are coming in. Guess who called me yesterday to say he'd be here?"

"Who?"

"Hank Rushmore."

"Old Tubby Rushmore?" Ben asked with a chuckle. "He was always crazy about you, Liz."

"My mother saw him last year and she says he's not fat anymore. He has his own computer firm now, in Wichita."

"It'll be good to see him," Ben said. He turned back to Ellie and his blue eyes had lost their twinkle. "Seriously, Ellie, you're pretty isolated out at the mill."

Ellie wished he'd mind his own business. "Not really. Pearl and Jake Vining are there mornings, and there are frequent customers. In fact, by the time five o'clock rolls around I'm usually ready to be alone for a while."

"I know the feeling," Liz commiserated.

"I wouldn't keep much money on hand, if I were you," Ben said, ignoring Liz's curious stare.

"I don't," Ellie said. "I'll be coming in to the bank several times a week."

Ben drummed his fingers on the checked tablecloth. "Do you see much of Oliver Hilderbrand?"

Ellie suspected it wasn't an idle question. "He comes after his mail almost every day."

"I wonder if you would give him a message for me. I haven't been able to reach him by phone."

"He doesn't have a phone at his cabin," Ellie said.

Ben hesitated before he went on. "I need a statement from him about his wife's death. It's just routine, but I'd like to take care of it as soon as possible. Would you ask him to come by the courthouse the next time he's in town?"

Liz was frowning. "Ben, is Mandy's death under investigation? I mean, is there any question—"

Ben cut in. "I said it's routine, Liz."

"But didn't you go out to the mill the day it happened?"

Ben took a swallow of his coffee before he answered. "Yes, but Doc Briar had given Hilderbrand a sedative, and he was in no condition to answer questions."

"I'll give him your message," Ellie said, wondering what was going on in Ben Stapleton's mind. She didn't know him well enough to guess. Yet she welcomed almost any topic of conversation that would get his mind off what had happened last night. "Pearl told me Mandy Hilderbrand drowned in the creek behind the mill house. Surely you don't suspect foul play."

"No," Ben said quickly. "I just want to close the case, for which I need Hilderbrand's statement."

Liz frowned. "Ellie, did Pearl suggest that it might not have been an accident?"

Ellie shook her head. "No, but she and Jake were reluctant to talk about it. After getting to know them a little better, I think the idea of an unnatural death, even an accidental one, disturbs them, especially Pearl. Sometimes I think she actually believes the mill is haunted. But Mr. Ingate warned me before I leased the mill that the hill people were superstitious about it." Ben was scrutinizing her, making her shift uneasily in her chair. "Pearl's certainly had the supernatural on her mind lately," Ellie went on. "She told me Priscilla Gunter's mental condition was caused by an encounter with a ghost." She managed to smile before adding, "A child ghost with blond curls. Pearl and her neighbors seem to think it was Mandy Hilderbrand's younger brother."

Liz's gray eyes widened. "Granny Gunter's senile. Surely Pearl realizes that." She made a dismissive gesture with her hand. "You can't pay any attention to the hill people's superstitions, Ellie. Those of us who were raised around here have heard ghost stories all our lives. It was a way of whiling away the long evenings before every little backwoods cabin had a television set."

"Mandy Hilderbrand's baby brother must have died thirty or forty years ago," Ellie said.

Liz looked perplexed. "No, it was only about three years ago, wasn't it, Ben?"

"But Mandy must have been middle-aged, at least, when she died," Ellie said.

Understanding came into Liz's gray eyes. "Oh. Naturally, you would assume that, because her husband's in his sixties. But Mandy was only nineteen, Ellie."

For some reason, this was disconcerting news to Ellie. "Really?" She had pictured the Hilderbrands as a couple in their latter years.

Liz nodded. "Mandy and Oliver Hilderbrand were certainly a unique pair."

"From what I hear, Mandy was always strange," Ben put in. "She was raised back in the hills by old man Swafford. He became almost a hermit after his wife died in childbirth, when William was born. Mandy took care of the baby. She couldn't have been more than fourteen when her mother died. Those two kids used to roam the woods like two wild animals. I don't think Mandy went to school much. Truant officers used to try to find her, but it's almost impossible to find the Swafford cabin unless you know the country well. And I suspect, if they ever did find it, they never found anybody home. I've heard Mandy always ran for the woods at the first sign of strangers."

Ben absently-mindedly rubbed the muscles at the back of his neck as he talked. Ellie said, "Pearl told me the Swafford baby was killed by coyotes."

"That was the general assumption," Liz said. "Little William just disappeared one day. His father thought he'd wandered off into the woods and got lost. He was used to going all over that part of the country with Mandy. The old man walked five miles to the nearest house and they organized a search party. Ben, that was right after you moved back here. Didn't you go out to help?"

Ben nodded. "We never found a sign of the child.

Wild animals seemed the only explanation." He flicked a glance in Ellie's direction. "Horrible way for a child to go."

A shiver skipped up Ellie's spine as she nodded wordlessly. Was he trying to frighten her?

After a moment, Liz said, "Mr. Swafford lived only a few weeks after that."

Ben added, "They found his body in the woods about a mile from his cabin. He'd been bitten by rattle-snakes."

Ellie shuddered visibly. She couldn't help it as she remembered her first morning at the mill when she had picked wildflowers and heard a slithering noise in the vines. Her hands, holding the cold glass, trembled. If Ben's intention was to scare her, he was succeeding.

"Mandy told the deputy who investigated," Ben said, "that her father had been drinking moonshine ever since William disappeared."

Liz sighed. "It was as if he was trying to drink himself to death. He must have passed out near a nest of rattlers. I guess you could say he really died of a broken heart."

"What happened to Mandy after that?" Ellie asked.

"There was some talk about trying to put her with a foster family," Ben said, "but she began to hide again whenever anyone came to the cabin. Nobody ever saw her, except maybe from a distance, running through the woods."

"But how did she live? What did she eat?"

"From fishing and hunting and planting a vegetable garden," Liz told her. "A couple of years ago, Oliver Hilderbrand came here from Missouri. He camped out in the woods. He wanted to buy the old Swafford mill and restore it. Mr. Swafford had let it fall down, hadn't operated it in years. I suppose that's how Hilderbrand got to know Mandy. She owned the mill. Maybe she trusted him because he was living in the woods, as she did. Anyway, first thing anyone knew, Hilderbrand had moved into the mill and started to repair it. Made it look better than it ever did when the Swaffords owned it. Then a few months back, he married Mandy."

As Liz finished speaking, Ben said abruptly, "Ellie, you probably should think about getting a gun."

Both Liz and Ellie looked at him in surprise. "Ben," Liz exclaimed, "are you trying to spook her?"

Liz's question echoed Ellie's thoughts. She was definitely getting the feeling that Ben Stapleton wanted to frighten her. Did he resent her living at the mill and want her to leave?

"Just the opposite," Ben said, holding Ellie's gaze. "When a woman lives alone in an isolated spot, it's wise to be prepared for even unlikely possibilities."

Ellie managed a shakey laugh. "I'm not sure whether you're warning me against burglars or ghosts."

Ben did not smile. "I'm suggesting that you exercise ordinary caution."

Ellie finished her drink before she replied. "I don't know one end of a gun from the other. Having one around would make me nervous."

Ben shifted restlessly in his chair. "I'm not trying to alarm you, but we do have our share of break-ins and thefts."

The sheriff's disclaimer to the contrary, Ellie thought he *was* trying to alarm her.

"You've probably heard that Priscilla Gunter's grandson was involved in a burglary at the high school."

"Pearl mentioned it. She seems to think Jimmy might go to jail."

Liz's dark brows arched disapprovingly. "Jimmy Gunter and the Crowder boys in jail? Ben, that would be a tragic mistake. Those kids have never had half a chance. Mrs. Crowder is trying to care for eight kids with a monthly welfare check. And Jimmy has no supervision from poor old Priscilla. Putting them in prison will only compound the problem. What they need is guidance."

"I agree," Ben said, "and I'm hoping the judge will grant probation. The trial won't come up for more than a month, though. If only they don't get into more trouble in the meantime. It might help if they'd tell what happened to the missing camera and tape recorders."

"Maybe they're afraid to," Liz speculated. "If they sold them, I mean. Isn't selling stolen property a separate offense?"

"Technically, yes," Ben agreed, "but in this case I doubt if it would make any difference to the outcome. The court has appointed an attorney for them. I'm going to talk to him. Maybe he can convince them to make a clean breast of it."

"Jimmy Gunter's been in the mill a couple of times," Ellie said. "He seems so shy. I can't imagine him breaking the law."

"They'd probably had a few beers," Ben said, "and one of the Crowder boys has admitted that it was his idea. The Crowders were involved in another break-in at the swimming pool summer before last. Jimmy just got carried along with the others."

Liz shook her head sadly. "Ben, I wouldn't have your job for anything. It's too depressing."

"Sometimes," he agreed. "Like today, for example. When I got to work this morning a man named Brohaugh, from Tulsa, was waiting for me. He's looking for his sixteen-year-old daughter. She ran away weeks ago. He's given up on the authorities and is searching for her himself. One of the girl's friends told him she might have headed this way. I tried to reassure him by telling him that nine times out of ten, runaways come home of their own accord. What I didn't say was that the longer they're gone, the less likely they'll turn up unharmed." He drained his coffee cup and got to his feet. "I've got to get back to work. Think about what I said, Ellie." His gaze flicked over her.

"I will," Ellie murmured, thinking that she had been at ease when she'd walked into the café with Liz and now she was strung tight. Ben gripped the back of his vacated chair and kept watching her. She struggled against an adolescent urge to tell him that he wasn't about to scare her out of the mill.

"Have you ever been on your own before?"

"That's hardly any concern of yours," she said, her temper flaring in spite of her best efforts to keep it in check.

"It is when I get hysterical phone calls in the middle of the night."

Her eyes flew angrily to his. "I wasn't hysterical. I've already apologized for waking you."

"I don't want your apologies. I just want you to think through what you're doing. Running the mill alone could turn into more than you bargained for."

Clearly he thought she was too fragile to meet the challenge. Well, it was true that she had never operated a business before. Mrs. Greg Harper's life had been frivolous and undemanding, and it was obvious that Ben Stapleton had a pretty fair picture of the kind of life she was used to. He was judging by appearances, and he had decided she was a shallow person. A manicured exterior with nothing of substance inside. Like Greg's friends. Was she really like that?

She pushed down a ripple of disappointment at Ben Stapleton's opinion of her. It didn't really matter what the sheriff thought. "You needn't worry about me," she said curtly, and after another moment he walked away.

"What was that about phone calls in the middle of the night?" Liz asked.

"It's embarrassing," Ellie said. "I thought I heard someone trying to break into the mill house last night, and I called him. It turned out to be nothing."

"It's natural that you'd be a little uneasy at first, living out there alone," Liz said. "I could kick Ben for that talk about guns and burglars. I think he's overly concerned. Did he upset you?"

"No," Ellie prevaricated. "He was just rubbing it in about last night. Well, I still have to go by the freight office before closing time." She glanced at her watch. "I'd hoped to get back to the mill before dark, but I won't make it now. I left Jake in charge and told him to lock up and go home at five if I hadn't gotten back."

They left the café together, separating on the sidewalk. "Give me a call the next time you feel uneasy," Liz said. "Talking to somebody else will help you put things in perspective."

After the freight office, Ellie stopped at the grocery store. It was almost seven when she got home. Dusk had settled like a gauzy gray blanket over the mill house and the surrounding woods. The clouds which had crowded the sky earlier in the day had dispersed, and a pale crescent moon was visible above the treetops.

Ellie let herself in and switched on a light. The place looked different—eerie almost—empty of people with the darkness pressing against the windows. The silence was so profound it seemed almost to be throbbing. The pulley and bins at the back lay in deep shadow and she was gripped by a flash of clawing panic. She remembered, as a child, coming into a dark house alone and having that same feeling. She had always had to look under every bed and into every closet before she could feel safe.

She walked slowly about the room, assuring herself that nothing was hiding in the shadowy corners. Then she went upstairs to the apartment and checked all the rooms there. Satisfied finally, she showered, donned a robe, and prepared a light supper for herself.

After placing the dirty dishes in the dishwasher, she wandered into the dark living room. Instead of switching on the television set, as she had intended, she stepped to the uncurtained window and looked out into the night. Stars glowed brightly in the evening sky, and the surrounding trees crowded together like black sentinels guarding the mill house. The peace was like a soothing balm to Ellie's spirit.

In spite of her denial, Ben's talk about break-ins and guns had unsettled her earlier. But now, standing at her living room window in the mill house, surrounded by the Ozark night, criminals and violence seemed very far away. She raised the window so that she could rest her elbows on the sill and let the cool breeze touch her face.

The sound of the croaking of frogs in the creek reached her, and night insect noises came to her on the soft sighing of the wind. She loved this place, and neither Ben Stapleton nor anyone else could quell this new feeling of contentment that was growing in her. She was making a new life for herself, a good life.

She stood there, hugging her velour robe about her against the autumn chill, becoming gradually bemused by the gentle sounds and smells of the night and the aura of peace. Then it seemed that she heard music, a melody far away, a voice singing. For one moment, as the wind rose and soughed through the trees, she almost thought she had caught some of the words.

". . . died . . . last night . . ."

A flicker of apprehension skipped up her spine. Suddenly the isolation of the mill seemed less comforting than frightening. Who could be singing in the woods after dark? As she stood there, such morbid thoughts went through her mind—thoughts of a girl hiding in the woods like a hunted animal, a baby killed by wild beasts, a young wife battered beneath the huge paddle wheel, spirits of the dead walking through the night.

The last thought made her laugh silently at herself. Ghosts, Ellie? Good grief!

It was patently absurd.

She remembered that her nearest neighbor was half a mile away and, realizing that a voice would not likely carry that far through the trees, she told herself it was only the wind she had heard. It couldn't be anything else.

It was getting colder. She shut the window and went in search of a book to read.

Chapter Five

The next day, Ben stopped by the mill on his way to work. Ellie was sorting the morning's mail when the front door opened, she looked up, and her eyes collided with his.

"Good morning, Sheriff," she said, turning her attention back to the mail. "What can I do for you?"

He leaned against the counter and made no immediate reply. As the silence stretched she looked up to meet his eyes before she realized that he was closer than she'd thought. His eyes were very blue and direct as they met hers, and then they drifted slowly down to her mouth, and back. "Did you deliver my message to Hilderbrand?"

She moved her shoulders to relieve a sudden tenseness. Why was a simple question making her pulse pound? "I haven't seen him yet. I probably will today and I'll tell him then."

"What do you think of him?"

"What?" She had to look up at him again, and something kindled inside her, something strong and only vaguely familiar. She hadn't felt this ill at ease around a man in years. And there was something else, too—a ripple of desire. But she didn't want to feel desire for any man, most certainly not this man.

"Hilderbrand."

She told herself the only reason she was affected by Ben Stapleton was that her emotional wounds hadn't fully healed.

"He's a nice man." She watched him rub a hand over his chin thoughtfully. "Soft-spoken. Private." Her eyes flew up again when Ben reached for a ballpoint pen lying between them and tapped it idly against the counter. For an instant, she had thought he was going to touch her.

She drew farther away from him and Ben, noticing her reaction, murmured, "You're jumpy this morning. Having trouble sleeping?"

"I sleep fine, thank you."

"Have you heard any more mice?"

"No." She turned away from him quickly, pretending to search the stamp drawer for something.

"Hey, Ben, I thought that was you." Jake came ambling toward the front, followed by Pearl.

Ellie could actually feel Ben's gaze leave her back as he greeted the Vinings. Her tenseness eased a little.

She closed the stamp drawer and turned around slowly. Jake was pumping Ben's hand.

"Got time for a cup of coffee, Ben?"

Ben darted a glance in Ellie's direction. "Sure."

Pearl was already lifting the coffeepot. "Want some, Ellie? There's enough here for everybody."

Ellie nodded and, feeling conspicuous standing there as the others sat down at the oak table, she slid into the vacant chair.

Jake said, "Couldn't help overhearing what you were saying about the reverend, Ben. Can't you give him a little more time to recover from his loss? Mandy's death, especially the way she died—it really hit him hard."

"I've already given him more time than I should have," Ben said.

Ellie had been trying for several days to find out exactly how long it had been since Oliver had lost his wife. Putting the question to the Vinings had proved frustratingly futile. "How long has it been since Mandy's death?"

"Three or four weeks now," Ben said.

"Three or four weeks!" She had been told that Mandy had died "recently," but she'd assumed that meant months, not weeks. Oliver must have decided to sell the mill immediately after Mandy died. For some strange reason, knowing that it had happened such a short time ago gave her an unsettled feeling.

Ben had lifted his coffee mug and was watching her over the rim. "Didn't you know?"

"Nobody ever told me," she murmured. "Not—not

that it makes any difference, I suppose. Only, it's hard to understand why Oliver Hilderbrand put the mill on the market so quickly. He loves this place. You ought to see the way he looks around at everything whenever he comes here."

Jake shook his head sadly. "I'll never forget that morning as long as I live."

"I wish you'd tell me about it, Jake," Ellie said.

"Oh, now," Pearl interrupted with a worried look, "I'm not so sure that's a good idea, Ellie."

"It's better than wondering," Ellie said.

Jake glanced at Ben, as if for permission. "If you're sure," Jake said uncertainly. Ellie nodded. "Well, I'm the one who saw her first. I'd just come to work that morning."

"Where was Oliver?" Ellie asked.

"Here, sacking up some meal. He was an early riser, they both were, and Mandy had a habit of leaving the mill before daybreak. She always did prefer the out of doors to four walls. Anyway, I was grinding corn when I happened to step to the back window and look out. I could see only a corner of her dress from here, so I went out to investigate. I—I had to tell the reverend and call the doc and Ben here."

"I still can't understand how it happened," Pearl said. "Mandy grew up around this mill. I can't believe she fell, or jumped either, for that matter."

"I hardly ever saw her," Jake stated, "even working here every day. She never did like to be around people much and, o' course, I'd been under the weather for more than a week and hadn't even been to work until that morning. But I'd have said she had sense enough not to fall under that wheel. She was surely strange, but she knew the danger of the wheel."

"That must have been dreadful for Mr. Hilderbrand," Ellie said, imagining the scene all too vividly.

"He was in a state, all right," said Jake. "First, he went outside and looked at her for a minute. When he came back, he looked like somebody had kicked him in the stomach. Just stood there wringing his hands, his mouth all twisted up. Then he started to moan and carry on. Kept saying, 'Mandy, Mandy, what have you done?'"

"That sounds as if he thought she did it deliberately," Ellie said.

Jake shrugged. "I wasn't even sure if he knew what he was saying. I was mighty glad when Doc Briar showed up and gave him a shot. Before he passed out, he made me promise we'd lay her out upstairs. Said he'd build her coffin himself and bury her beside her folks."

The old man squinted nearsightedly at the hands wrapped around his mug. How well *could* he see, Ellie wondered. "Jake, you said you saw her from the back window. How? I mean . . ."

Jake peered at her with an understanding grin. "Oh, I can't see so well, that's true. But the minute I glimpsed that spot of white, I knew it was Mandy. She didn't have many frocks and she wore that white dress half the time. I'd see her passing up the stairs or going out the door in it. I'd have known that dress anywhere. When I saw that spot of white floating on the water, I knew. Besides, there was all that long, yellow hair floating out from under the wheel. Hope I never see anything like it again."

Ellie glanced from Jake to Pearl. They both looked uncomfortable. Even Ben refused to meet her eyes. She remembered that Pearl had once started to tell her something about Mandy's being caught under the mill wheel. "I want to know it all," she said determinedly.

"Ellie, no," protested Pearl.

"Yes," she persisted.

"I'll tell you if you insist," Ben said after a long pause. "Somebody's bound to mention it to you sooner or later, anyway. Mandy got her head caught under the wheel. When Jake and I pulled her out, her . . . her face was gone."

Ellie's hand flew to her mouth. "Oh, no!" she whispered. "How horrible!" Pearl was looking at her hands. For an irrational moment, Ellie wished she hadn't pressed them to tell her. Would she ever be able to look at the mill wheel again without imagining that battered face beneath it? It had been a tragic accident, to be sure, but was it enough to account for the Vinings' unease every time the subject of Mandy's death came up? "Could she have been pushed? Did she have any enemies?"

"That's what Ben asked me that day," Jake said. "Funny question when it came to Mandy. Nobody knew her well enough to be an enemy, or a friend. Mandy lived in a world all her own. It was almost like she wasn't really flesh and blood." He shrugged. "No, she never talked to nobody except her husband. How could she have any enemies?"

"What do you think, Ben?" Ellie asked.

"I didn't even know Mandy," Ben said. "I'd heard about her, but she was never around when I stopped by the mill. I'd never even seen her until the day she died."

"I'll always think it was the jinx," Jake mused.

Ellie looked at the old man questioningly. "The jinx?"

"The Swaffords were jinxed," Jake said matter-of-factly, "the whole family. The minute I saw that white dress, I knew it was the jinx."

"But that's just superstition . . ." Ellie began before she thought how it might sound.

Ben caught her eye and moved his head in a barely perceptible shake. Protecting his own people from what he perceived as Ellie's kind. "I'm sorry, Jake. I really don't know anything about the Swaffords."

Pearl spoke then in a sorrowful voice. "She didn't deserve to die like that. She never hurt nobody that I know of, even though she was queer-acting and all. It was just Mandy's time to go, I guess."

"Speaking of goin'," Jake said, getting to his feet, "we better get to work, woman."

When the Vinings had moved away, Ellie said defensively, "I didn't mean to insult Jake."

"These people might have unusual beliefs," Ben said, "but they're very proud. They don't cotton to city slickers laughing at them."

Ellie got to her feet abruptly and walked back to the post office counter. Ben followed her, leaning over to watch her. He made her so nervous! "Honestly," she breathed in a low voice that the Vinings couldn't hear.

"Ghosts and jinxes and haunted mills! You don't believe any of that, do you?"

He smiled crookedly. "At one time I'd have answered a flat no to that question, but lately I wonder sometimes. I've heard some weird tales from these hill people, things that are hard to explain from natural causes. One thing I'm sure of, they think they're supernatural." He paused, seeing Ellie's stricken look. "Sorry, Ellie. I forgot for a moment how skittish you are. I was just kidding."

Skittish! The man never lost an opportunity to remind her of that mouse. She sniffed and began to stuff the morning's mail into the letter boxes.

"Your sense of humor escapes me."

He chuckled. "What do you do on Sundays?"

She tucked a final letter into its box and looked at him sharply. "Why?"

"The mill is closed on Sundays, and I just wondered what you do with yourself?"

She lifted her shoulders. "Bake. Read. Whatever strikes my fancy."

"Would you come to my place for an early dinner next Sunday?"

Ellie let out an annoyed breath. "Why? So you can try to scare the living daylights out of me again?"

He lifted a brow and waited a beat. "If I've scared you, it wasn't intentional. I was under the impression you didn't need any help in that department. But I'd like to talk about Hilderbrand some more."

She didn't know how to react. If only she had an inkling as to what his real motives were. "Then you should find someone who knows the man."

"That's just the problem. Nobody knows him very well. But since you're an outsider you might have noticed something the others missed."

Outsider. She hated that word, but she had the feeling that she would always be an outsider to Ben Stapleton. The thought outraged her. She was making a place for herself here! She wouldn't be an outsider for long, and she didn't care what the sheriff thought about it. There was a quick sense of panic at the idea of going to Ben's house, being alone with him. She squelched it instantly, viciously. She mustn't let him guess that he affected her so strongly. "What time?"

"Six? I'll drive over for you."

"Never mind. I'll drive myself."

He studied her thoughtfully for an instant. "Okay. If you change your mind, give me a call."

He left the mill, ran down the steps outside, and got into his car. For a few moments, he sat behind the wheel, making no move to start the engine, getting some home truths straight in his mind. He was mightily attracted to Ellie Harper, and he didn't know quite what to do about it. She wasn't like the other women he'd known.

He had asked her to dinner Sunday. The realization struck him fully as he drove away. What had possessed him? He wanted to talk about Hilderbrand, he'd told her, but that was just an excuse. He didn't really think she knew any more about the old man than he did. Eleanor Harper wasn't his kind, but she continued to intrigue him. Maybe because of those brief glimpses of something beneath that aloof exterior. She was running away from something. She had been hurt and had gone into hiding. He sensed it. The cop in him wanted to know what could send a woman like Ellie to a place like this.

Ellie was busy with customers most of the afternoon and didn't have time to think about Ben or what she'd learned that morning about Mandy's death.

Since it was Wednesday, Oliver Hilderbrand brought his van to the mill, as promised. He refused her offer of a lift back to his cabin and disappeared into the woods on foot.

At five o'clock she locked up and went upstairs. She knew that she had to keep her mind occupied or she would start thinking about Mandy and the horrible way she'd died. Or, what was hardly less troubling, Ben Stapleton and why he had invited her to his home for dinner.

She made a meatloaf and put it into the oven with a potato to bake. Then she mixed cookie dough for baking when the meatloaf was done.

Later, she carried her dinner into the living room and sat by the window to eat, watching as the evening shadows gradually enclosed the woods and the mill house. She sat there until it was too dark to see and the silence seemed filled with small, unfamiliar sounds.

Just to have some noise in the apartment, she turned on the television set. A movie she'd been wanting to see came on, and she became engrossed in it. After the movie she showered and put on a nightgown. She turned off all the lights except the bedside lamp and settled herself in bed to read a historical novel by a favorite author. She would keep all frightening thoughts at bay by reading until she could fall asleep.

But she'd only read a few pages in the novel when a loud noise shuddered through the silence, making her start convulsively and drop the book. Her heart leaped and pounded in her ears. For a few moments she sat there, paralyzed.

It sounded like a low rumbling of thunder, except it kept going on and on. Finally she was able to move and got out of bed. Softly, she padded out of the bedroom and across the living room to the apartment door, which she had locked securely when she came upstairs.

She realized then that the sound was coming from below. She looked over her shoulder at the telephone. But she couldn't call Ben, not after the last time. Her trembling hands reached for the bolt and pulled it back soundlessly. Slowly she opened the door a crack.

She peered out into the darkness. The loud, rumbling sound continued. She knew that she had locked the doors downstairs and checked all the windows to make sure they were locked. No one could possibly be inside the mill house.

Taking courage from this thought, she stepped onto the landing and flipped the switch that turned on the lights downstairs. The noise went on, seeming to grow louder as she crossed the landing. She hesitated there, looking down the stairs and craning to see what she could of the first floor. It wasn't much—a small section of wall and about half of the front door. It was still closed.

She could call Liz, but what could Liz do nine miles away? Call Ben, her fearful heart hammered. He would ask her if she'd been downstairs to investigate, and she would have to say no. . . . And what if he came and found nothing? She would have cried wolf the second time, and he'd never take her seriously again. He already believed she jumped at every shadow.

As she stood there in an agony of indecision, it suddenly dawned on her what the noise was. If she hadn't been so frightened, she would have realized it right away. It was the paddle wheel in the creek in back of the mill.

But how could it have been turned on? The only switch controlling it was inside the locked mill house.

She couldn't move. It felt as if her bare feet had turned to lead. She opened her mouth to call out—but her throat was so tight with fear that she couldn't make a sound.

Someone had gotten inside the mill house and turned on the paddle wheel—someone or some*thing* . . .

Chapter Six

Something's inside! The words echoed in her mind like a shout reverberating from tall canyon walls. The grind of the paddle wheel went on, and the vibrations it made traveled from the floor through the soles of her bare feet.

Ellie gripped the door facing and tried to think. Whoever was downstairs—it had to be a *person;* she wouldn't entertain the absurdity of ghosts or wild beasts. A person was bad enough—whoever, knew that she was there; she had given herself away by turning on the downstairs lights. So she had to call his bluff. If she was going to die, let her die standing up for herself, not cowering in a corner.

"You, downstairs!" she called out, and the strong

sound of her voice over the rumbling wheel steadied her a little. "I have a gun. I'll give you exactly one minute to clear out before I come down these stairs shooting!"

She went back into her apartment, locking the door behind her. Quaking, she scrambled into jeans, a shirt, and shoes. She would feel a little less vulnerable fully clothed. Then she hefted a heavy vase from the kitchen, but her fragile courage deserted her at the last minute.

She went to the phone and dialed Ben's number. She let it ring seven or eight times before she hung up. He wasn't home, and she didn't know if she was relieved or desolated by his absence. But knowing that Ben wouldn't be coming narrowed her options to one. She had to face whoever was downstairs alone.

Clutching the vase, she unlocked the apartment door again and started quietly down the stairs. The intruder wouldn't be able to hear her over the sound of the paddle wheel, and at least she would have the element of surprise in her favor. She might even be able to slip out the front door and get into her car before he saw her. But she hadn't brought the car keys with her!

She hesitated, already more than halfway down the stairs, wondering if she should go back for the keys. But as long as she was so far down, she might as well try to get a glimpse of what she was up against. She bent so that she could see most of the ground floor.

Everything was exactly as she had left it; she saw no one. For a few moments she stood still, hearing the thunder of her heart in her ears almost as loudly as the relentless rumble of the paddle wheel. Her eyes searched the room from front to back. No one was there.

She crept the rest of the way down the stairs, still holding the vase in both hands in front of her. At the bottom of the steps she had a clear view of every corner of the room. She was alone in the mill house.

Suddenly energized, she ran across the room to the back wall and pulled down on the switch controlling the paddle wheel. The ensuing silence was thick, unbroken, and wonderful.

In the stillness, Ellie's leather heels against the bare oak floor sounded as loud as pistol shots as she moved about the room, rechecking all the windows and doors. Everything was securely locked.

All at once the adrenalin drained out of her, and she felt limp. She sagged back against the front door and tried to puzzle out how the wheel could have been turned on when everything was locked up as tight as a drum.

Could she possibly have failed to lock one of the doors before going upstairs, allowing someone to come inside, turn on the wheel, and leave, locking the door behind him? It was even possible that somebody had a key. Even so, that didn't explain why. Why would somebody want to frighten her? To make her pack up and leave the mill house? The only person who could logically have a key that she didn't know about was Oliver Hilderbrand, and he was the one person she couldn't believe was trying to frighten her away. No one had forced him to lease her the place; he had chosen to do so without even waiting to see if he received any better offers. He also had told her that the key he'd given her, along with the one she'd gotten from Barney Ingate, were the only keys to the mill house. She'd given the spare to the Vinings. If someone had come inside tonight, she couldn't believe it was Oliver Hilderbrand—and certainly not either of the Vinings. So where did that leave her?

It was remotely possible that there was an electrical short in the line or behind the switch which had caused the switch to be turned on.

These were the only explanations she could think of, and none of them was very probable. Finally, she climbed back upstairs, remembering what she had called from above before coming down.

I'll give you exactly one minute to clear out before I come down these stairs shooting. Good heavens, Ellie! Imagining herself barreling down the stairs with a smoking gun in each hand struck her as hilariously funny, now that the danger had turned out to be unreal. She laughed aloud as she reached the second floor landing and entered the apartment. She felt a definite satisfaction, too. She'd had the nerve to go downstairs and face whatever she had to face. She'd discovered courage in herself. It made her feel proud.

She returned the vase to the kitchen, still chuckling and shaking her head. She didn't need a gun! There was a perfectly logical explanation for the things that had frightened her since she moved into the mill house. First there had been the mouse. And, although the explanation for tonight's adventure was less obvious, she was sure that whatever it was, it wasn't sinister. She was glad Ben hadn't answered his telephone. If he wasn't convinced already that she was hysterical, he would've been after this.

As she got ready for bed again, she told herself it was just as well that she was making deliveries the next day. It would do her good to get away from the mill house. A change in routine was probably all she needed. That and a little more time to settle into her new life.

Almost twenty-four hours later, Ellie returned, with a new batch of orders to be filled, having driven more than four hundred miles. She'd decided to make the deliveries herself one more time, but she could see that she would have to ship the orders after that. It was a nice thought to get to know her customers personally, but it just wasn't practical. She'd be on the road two or three days a week if she tried to do it.

It had been a satisfying and prosperous trip, but she was glad to be home. The Vinings had left the downstairs lights on for her, Ellie noticed gratefully as she brought the van to a stop in front of the mill house. Its yellow rectangular windows in the Ozark night welcomed her warmly. Sighing, she got out of the van and went inside.

Rejuvenated by a shower and a bowl of vegetable soup, Ellie found that she wasn't sleepy. On a sudden impulse, she put on her warm velour robe and house shoes and went out to sit on the front steps. A slight breeze had whipped up within the last few minutes, and it wafted the faint smell of rain to Ellie's nostrils. She leaned her head against the railing and breathed deeply. It was raining off to the east. She wondered if it was coming her way, and hoped that it was. How she had enjoyed, as a child, sitting on her grandparents' front porch, wrapped in a quilt, while it rained. Funny, she hadn't thought of that in years. The air-conditioned house in Houston hadn't even had a porch for sitting on while it rained. And even if it had, her neighbors would have thought her daft. It had seemed important then, what the Harpers' sophisticated neighbors thought. Now she knew how little their opinions mattered.

The delicate aroma of some sweet-smelling flower wafted past, and she heaved a deep sigh of contentment. This place was so peaceful, so incredibly lovely that it brought the quick, hot sting of tears to her eyes. Surprised, she wiped her eyes with the back of her hand. The counselor had warned her that her emotions were still very close to the surface, but crying over the smell of wild flowers was ridiculous!

For a few moments she lost herself in imagining that she was the only person for miles and miles. But the fantasy was broken when she heard the muffled sound of a car passing on a nearby road.

The sound grew dimmer as the car moved farther away. And then she heard another sound that seemed to come from even farther off, the faint sound of a female voice, singing. She could hear only enough to know that the voice was high and as clear as one of the Ozarks' rocky streams.

Ellie turned her face toward the breeze, for the singing seemed to come from that direction. She listened and listened until she thought she could make out some of the words: "Sweet William died for me last night . . ."

Then the singing trailed away and was gone. Afterward, she couldn't even be sure that she had heard a woman singing. Perhaps she had only heard the wind whining through the trees. More likely, the driver of the car that had passed nearby had had his windows open and the radio on.

A car radio was the explanation Ellie had settled on when she remembered what Pearl had said about Priscilla Gunter wandering around outside at night. Had she heard old Priscilla singing?

Well, whatever it was, she could no longer hear it. Except for the frail sighing of the wind, all was still. The silent darkness soothed her like a satin balm. She sat on, her head still resting against the railing, her eyelids growing heavier, until a drop of rain splattered on her hand and drowsiness drove her inside to bed.

The next two days, Friday and Saturday, would be the busiest of the week if this week followed last week's pattern. But Sunday would be quiet, with dinner at Ben's house. Ellie wasn't even aware of the tentative smile that softened her mouth as she thought about Ben.

Warm wood tones everywhere. Bright braided rugs. Well-worn overstuffed furniture. Ellie looked around with keen interest as Ben led her through his den and into a big, country kitchen. Houses spoke to Ellie. Each one had its own special ambience. Ben's house felt relaxed, comfortable.

"I heard you coming, so I poured us some wine." He handed her a stemmed glass of rich ruby liquid, then opened the oven door to check what smelled deliciously like barbecued meat.

"Ribs," he said over his shoulder. "I hope you like them."

"Love them," Ellie murmured, sipping the smooth burgundy.

Ben closed the oven door. Ellie wore a dress of a lavender fabric so soft it seemed to float around her, and as Ben straightened he looked at her with male appreciation in his eyes.

"You look lovely," he said simply. "That color suits you."

Ellie felt her cheeks warming with pleasure and forgot that Ben had asked her to dinner to talk about Oliver Hilderbrand. She lifted her eyes to his. "Thank you." She was thinking that she would've been wiser not to have come there at all. "You have an attractive place here."

Ben smiled, but he sounded almost grave as he said, "I like it." She's being very cautious, he thought. Alert. Watchful. Like a bird who has been startled by a sudden noise. She's distrustful, he realized, and wondered why.

He set himself the task of putting her at ease. He took the ribs from the oven and removed them to a large white platter, which he set on the table at one end of the kitchen. The table was spread with a crisp red cloth and set with white pottery. "Nice little showers we've had the past two nights," he remarked conversationally. "We needed rain." Reduced to talking about the weather? he chided himself silently. You're a great conversationalist, Stapleton.

"Yes."

"Would you get the salads from the refrigerator?"

She placed two bowls of salad greens beside the two plates while Ben got the bowl of creamed corn from the stove and a loaf of buttered wheat bread from the oven.

They sat down and Ben said, "I always seem to be able to sleep better when it's raining." God, why couldn't he think of something besides the weather to talk about?

"Ummm. I know what you mean."

"Does it rain much in Houston?" he asked casually.

"Quite a bit. It's very humid."

"Didn't you like living there?"

Ellie raised her eyes. They had become very cool. Private. "It was all right, except for the traffic. I like it better here."

What was her ex-husband like? he wondered suddenly. A business executive. A lawyer, perhaps. Somebody successful, well-heeled. Somebody just right for Eleanor Harper, so what had happened?

"Why here?" he inquired, studying Ellie's face.

"My grandparents lived near here," Ellie said. "I used to visit them as a child." She lifted a piece of lettuce on her fork and ate it slowly before she said, "They've been dead for several years, but I always thought I would like to come back."

She was happy here once, Ben mused with a sudden spark of insight, that's what she came back for. She hasn't been happy for some time.

"Where are your parents?"

"My father died when I was ten. My mother and stepfather live in Oregon. I don't see them often."

"You aren't close to your mother?"

"I didn't say that." Ellie took a sip of wine. She wished he wouldn't watch her so intently. He seemed to be adept at reading body language. How else could he have guessed that she and her mother were like two strangers? Her mother had said on the telephone that Ellie was crazy to give up Greg and the lifestyle he provided without a fight. When Ellie insisted that she no longer wanted Greg or the lifestyle, her mother's advice was to "take him to the cleaners." He wanted to marry another woman? Let him pay through the nose for it. Hadn't Ellie worked to help put him through his residency? When Ellie said that she was satisfied with the house and her car, her mother had called her stupid and hung up on her. They had talked on the telephone once since the divorce, but they hadn't found much to say to each other and the conversation had been brief.

A drop of wine lingered at the corner of her mouth as she set her glass down, and the tip of her tongue came out to claim it. The unconscious little tableau aroused Ben. "What does your ex-husband do?"

Ellie let out an annoyed breath. "Ben—"

"Just trying to get to know you."

She lifted a brow and waited for a beat. "He's a plastic surgeon."

"A doctor. I should've guessed."

Ellie laughed. It was the first time he'd heard her laugh, and the tinkling sound delighted him. "Why should you have guessed?"

"You look like a doctor's wife," Ben pointed out,

and unexpectedly reached across the table to link his fingers with hers. "Soft. Well cared for. Used to nice things."

She drew her hand away. "I'm not a doctor's wife now. I operate a gristmill."

"How long were you married?"

She wasn't used to such unabashed curiosity. It wasn't rudeness, though she had an impulse to retort angrily. And it wasn't casual, which perhaps explained the extreme defensiveness she was feeling.

"Nine years," Ellie said uncomfortably. His eyes never left hers. She put some of the steaming ribs onto her plate. "Forgive me, but I'm going to use my fingers. I can't seem to eat ribs any other way."

Her neat, white teeth separated a sliver of meat from the bone, making Ben smile. Somehow he knew that Dr. Harper's wife would never have eaten with her fingers in front of anybody. "Is there any other way to eat ribs?" He followed her example, eating with gusto.

"Umm, delicious," Ellie murmured as she deposited the bone on her plate and wiped her slender fingers on her napkin. "You're a good cook, Ben."

"A bachelor has to be."

"Why haven't you ever married?"

"I thought about it once."

"With Liz Pembrook?" The flash of surprise in Ben's eyes made her smile. "Pearl Vining told me you and Liz dated for a long time."

"Yeah, Liz and I used to talk about marriage." He grinned suddenly—a quick grin that crinkled lines at the corners of his eyes. "We started going steady when we were seventeen. Eventually I moved to Fayetteville to work for the highway patrol. When I came home three years ago, neither Liz nor I had found anyone else, so we sort of took up where we'd left off. It was an easy habit to slip back into, taking each other for granted. Finally we realized we liked each other a lot, but we weren't in love, so we called it quits. It was a mutual decision."

Ellie felt a tingle of unexpected warmth. Pearl was wrong; Liz hadn't broken Ben's heart. Why she should feel grateful for this, she couldn't have said. She lifted her glass. It must be the wine that was making her feel so giddy.

After they'd finished eating, she helped Ben clear the table and fill the dishwasher. Then they went into the big, pine-paneled den. Ben sat down on the sofa. Ellie hesitated for a moment before sitting beside him. It would look odd if she sat in the chair halfway across the room.

"I'd better be getting back home," she said.

"Relax for a few minutes. It's early yet."

She settled into the corner of the sofa, drawing her legs up beneath her full skirt. "I thought about walking over, but since I'm not familiar with the countryside yet, I decided to wait and explore it by daylight."

"You should never go walking alone at night. There are rattlesnakes around here. Not to mention a few cliffs and sudden drop-offs. You could lose your footing and fall before you even knew you were in danger."

"Cliffs?"

He nodded. "There's one about a quarter-mile west of the mill. If you don't know it's there, it's hard to see it coming on it from above. Last winter a hunter fell off it and broke both his legs. He was lucky it didn't kill him."

"I'll certainly confine my walking to the daytime hours then." Ben's words seemed to have brought a sense of danger into the room. She wondered if he felt it, too.

Taking her completely by surprise, he ran his finger down the back of her hand. "Had any more problems at the mill house?" His fingertips were warm; they made her flesh tingle.

She darted a quick look into his face before glancing away. He wasn't laughing at her this time. "Nothing serious. The other night, the paddle wheel switch got turned on and the noise woke me."

"How did that happen?" he inquired, and lifted her hand to his lips.

Trembling a little, she removed her hand from his. Her fingers burned with a strange heat. "That's the odd part. The switch is inside, and the mill house was locked. When I went downstairs, there was nobody there and the wheel was going full force." She shook her head and the shining auburn waves bounced on her shoulders. "A small mystery for you to puzzle over in your spare time, Sheriff."

He reached for her hand again. "A piece of cake. You left a door unlocked and somebody—a kid probably—thought it would be a good joke." He enclosed her hand securely in both of his and gave her an artless smile. "Jimmy Gunter, do you think?"

Ellie glanced at their hands, then aimed a thoughtful look at Ben. "No. I checked all the locks before I went upstairs and again after the paddle wheel was turned on."

Ben hesitated a moment. "Are you sure?"

He seemed to be closer to her than before, but she hadn't seen him move. She made an effort to keep her voice cool and even. "Of course, I'm sure." Didn't he believe her? "Why would you ask me that?"

He was so close to her that she could feel his breath fanning her cheek. "Sometimes people are sure they've done something when actually they haven't, especially if it's something they do every day, like locking up before going to bed."

She jerked her hand away. "Well, I know I locked everything before I went upstairs," she said hotly. "Don't be condescending with me, Ben Stapleton!"

"Relax, Ellie." His hands clasped her shoulders firmly. "I'm not being condescending. I see it happen all the time."

"Not this time."

Her shoulders felt so thin and fragile. He had an urge to press her closer until she melted into him. "Since you seem to have discarded the idea of a ghost," he said, smiling when she shot him a speaking look, "then somebody has a key."

"There are only two keys. I have one, and the Vinings have the other."

"Maybe Hilderbrand kept one."

Ellie drew away from him slightly, confused by the tingling thrills that rippled along her skin. "I thought of that. But even if he did, why would he come in and turn on the paddle wheel? It doesn't make sense."

His eyes followed her hand as it smoothed the lavender dress over her legs. Until now he hadn't been willing to admit to himself his reason for asking Ellie to dinner tonight. To talk about Hilderbrand, he'd said. Bull! He wanted to touch her again. His body stirred with arousal from the feel of her body under his hands. He had never wanted a woman so badly, nor been as certain that she wasn't for him. He couldn't even be sure she wasn't imagining these strange occurrences in the middle of the night. Or making them up to get attention. Unfolding his long frame, he stood, to put some distance between them. To keep his hands from betraying him again, he shoved them into his trousers pockets. "Could Hilderbrand be regretting your contract? Has he said anything to you about it?"

She looked up at him with an uncertain expression. "No. He's a gentle, kind man. I can't believe he'd resort to such childish tricks. Anyway, he's never given me any indication that he regrets our agreement. I gave him your message, by the way. He said he'd get in touch with you."

"He hasn't."

"Well, he hasn't had much time yet. I'm sure he'll come to see you the next time he's in town."

He frowned as he walked to an overstuffed armchair and braced himself against its back. "If he doesn't, I'll track him down." He dismissed the subject with a shrug of his shoulders. "Ellie . . ." He hesitated for a moment and his eyes held hers. "If the mill house was locked and nobody but the Vinings has another key, how could the switch have been turned on? Could you have dreamed it?"

He didn't believe her! She got abruptly to her feet. "I know the difference between dreams and reality, Sheriff." She was looking around for the straw bag she had brought with her, and saw finally that it had slipped down beside the cushion of the chair behind which Ben was standing. She took a few steps and snatched up the bag. "Thank you for dinner," she muttered grudgingly as she started for the door.

"Ellie, wait!" With a few long strides, he caught up with her and turned her to face him. "Why are you always so defensive?"

She started to draw away. "I have to go."

"No, you don't." He slid his arms around her. "I'm sorry if I've insulted you."

This man thinks you're slightly cracked, Ellie, she told herself. Surely you aren't going to let him hold you. But she said nothing, and she didn't resist as he pressed her closer.

His eyes drifted to her mouth. "I've been thinking about kissing you ever since you walked in the door tonight." Lightly, his lips brushed over hers.

Don't you have any pride at all, Ellie? her mind demanded. Apparently not, for she didn't turn away as his mouth crushed hers.

Something sprang up between them—quick, hot, demanding—and Ellie was caught in its onslaught, stunned by his sudden passion and her own instant response. There wasn't time for thinking, only reacting. Her lips parted. Her hands found his waist and crept around to his back.

The need was so strong that they were both helpless to do anything but try to assuage it. Such urgency was unknown to Ellie. Had this hunger to taste and touch been in her all her life? Her mouth, soft with passion, almost drove him over the edge of reason, and he felt his control slipping away. He moaned, and when his hand caressed her breast through the thin lavender fabric, there was an answering moan from her.

Ellie's sanity had flown. She needed the intimacy of his tongue staking claim to her mouth, his strong hands searching her body. She needed his strength, and she felt in him a matching need. It terrified her. Need for another person was a trap that she must avoid at all costs. She was just learning to take care of herself. The risks of needing somebody else were too great.

"No." Ellie wrenched her mouth from his in a sudden panic. "No," she repeated, and somehow she found the strength to draw away.

His hands fell to his sides as he looked down at her. The hot desire in his eyes mingled with a turmoil that she didn't understand. He sounded almost angry when he said roughly, "Why, Ellie?" But even as he said it, he fought against the pounding need inside him, disgusted with himself. He hadn't expected the violent hunger that had churned to the surface the moment his mouth touched hers.

"I have to go." Ellie looked behind her for the door, for the way out.

"What are you afraid of?"

There was no point in denying that she was afraid. Ellie took a deep breath. "I don't want to feel . . . the way you make me feel. I'm afraid of—of losing myself." With a lift of her shoulders, she turned her back on him and walked quickly out the door.

Ben thrust his hands in his pockets to keep them from reaching out for her. He clamped his jaw shut to keep from calling to her to come back.

"You're a fine one to accuse her of being afraid, Stapleton," he muttered. "That woman scares the hell out of you."

With restless feet, he wandered through his house, thinking about Ellie, wondering . . . Who was she? The sophisticated, possibly shallow person she appeared to be, or the warm, passionate woman he'd held in his arms for a few moments tonight? Why had she come here? And was somebody trying to terrorize her, or was she a paranoid with a wildly vivid imagination?

Chapter Seven

Lying in her bed in the dark, Ellie was doing her share of wondering. Ben hadn't really believed that the mill wheel had started running in the middle of the night. He thought she'd dreamed it, which must mean he thought her unstable. Was she? Could she have had a dream so real that she convinced herself it really happened? The question lingered in the dark silence to mock her.

Disquieted, she turned on her side in the bed, drawing her pillow down between her arms and her knees up to meet it, as if to protect herself from unexpected blows. It had happened, damn it! Ben was judging by appearances, just as her old Houston set did. He had labeled her that first day when he'd given her the traffic ticket, classified her as everything she had been trying to get away from when she left Texas. Okay, so sometimes she still slipped into her old social persona when she was nervous, but inside she wasn't that person at all.

It made her so angry that Ben couldn't see beyond the facade! She would not accept other people's labels anymore. If Ben chose to see only the surface, then that's what he would see. But it didn't make Ben right. There wasn't a thing she could do about Ben's misperception, so she refused to let it upset her.

It had been a mistake to tell him about the wheel. She'd been fooled into misplaced confidence by the wine and the intimacy. Perhaps that had been his plan. It humiliated her to remember how she had responded to his kiss.

"I don't want to feel anything for Ben," she said aloud. Weariness settled over her all at once. Where had those feelings come from and so quickly? Would she have felt them if another man had kissed her? she wondered. The questions continued to nag inside her for a long time. She was deeply troubled by something she couldn't quite pinpoint. It kept her awake, turning restlessly.

The ringing of the phone startled her, and she sat upright in the bed as she reached for the extension on the bedside table.

"Ellie? I haven't called too late, have I?" It was Liz Pembrook.

Ellie relaxed, resting her cheek on the pillow. "No, not at all."

"I called earlier but you weren't there."

"I went out for a while."

"I was wondering if we could have lunch tomorrow. There's a good Mexican place south of town."

"I'd like to." Liz's invitation made her feel better, less isolated. "I have to come in to the bank, anyway. I could pick you up at your shop at twelve."

"Good. I'll look forward to it. Ellie . . . is everything all right? You sound odd."

"It's nothing I can't handle."

Liz was silent for a long moment before she said, "Okay. See you tomorrow then."

Ellie replaced the receiver. Liz's voice had brought the outside world into the mill house and with it, perspective. She was, Ellie decided, making too much of what had happened between her and Ben.

Maybe she could sleep now. As she closed her eyes and burrowed deeper into her pillow, she became aware of a faint sound, the same scratching noise that she had heard once before. She turned her head and listened intently. The sound came from below. That mouse was still between the foundation walls, trying to get out. You'd think he would have starved to death by now.

She wouldn't let it disturb her, she resolved as she turned back on her side and covered her ears with her hands. But she couldn't close out the sound completely. Finally it stopped, and she was able to go to sleep.

She was up early the next morning. Her eyes reflecting back at her from the bathroom mirror were shadowed. She applied makeup to the shadows and went outside for a walk before time to open the mill. She crossed the creek by way of the bridge behind the mill house to stroll along the bank and watch the water rush past. The silver, ripply surface reminded her of semi-transparent crushed velvet.

Coming back the way she had gone, she saw that the trees on the rim of the hill had more gold in them than they had the last time she'd noticed. Among the gold an occasional tree was beginning to turn orange or blood red, and a blue haze hung over the valley beyond the nearest hills. Autumn in the Ozarks was as incredibly beautiful as the color postcards for sale in Springville's souvenir shops.

The nights were growing crisp and cool, but the morning's golden sunshine warmed Ellie through the long sleeves of her shirt as she turned back toward the bridge. To reach the front door, she walked around the north side of the mill house. Near the back corner, where the stone foundation was four feet high, she noticed bits of a white substance scattered on the ground. She halted to examine the white specks more closely. Looking straight on at the foundation from her squatting position, she could see marks around several of the stones, as if something had been used to scrape away some of the mortar, which lay in white flakes at her feet. Her fingers traced around one of the stones, feeling the rough, scraped mortar, before she stood.

A frown creased her brow. How strange. Did termites ever attack mortar? Or was there some other insect that did?

All at once, she remembered hearing that scratching noise during the night. The first time she'd heard it, when Ben had come to investigate, they had traced the sound to this wall. Could a mouse inside the foundation have knocked that much mortar loose? It didn't seem possible.

An odd shiver passed through her, but she shook it off as she went inside. When the Vinings arrived, Ellie took Jake outside to show him the damaged mortar.

"Do you have any idea what could have caused it?" she asked as Jake bent close to peer nearsightedly at the foundation.

He straightened, shaking his head. "Beats me."

"Could it be a rat inside the foundation?"

"Rats are destructive creatures, but I can't picture a rat doing that. 'Pears to me the mortar's been loosened from the outside. Next time you're in town, get me a sack of cement, and I'll fix it."

"I think I'd better get some rat poison, too," Ellie said as they went back inside the mill together.

Pearl was sacking cornmeal, singing a mournful-sounding song. As Ellie and Jake approached, Ellie was able to make out some of the words over the rumble of the paddle wheel.

> *"Mother, Mother, make my bed.*
> *Make it long and narrow.*
> *Sweet William died for me last night.*
> *I'll die for him tomorrow."*

Ellie halted in her tracks behind the other woman. "Pearl?"

Pearl jumped and turned to Ellie with a laugh. "Law, I didn't hear you comin', Ellie. Nearly jumped outa my skin."

Ellie put her hand on Pearl's arm. "I'm sorry, but that song you were singing. What is it?"

Pearl set a full sack of cornmeal aside and reached for another. "That was Mandy's song."

"What do you mean, it was Mandy's song—did she make it up?"

"Oh, no. It's a common old song. My mother used to sing it. I think of it as Mandy's song because she sang it all the time. She'd walk through the woods singing it over and over. I heard her many times."

"She sang it around the mill, too," Jake said. "There was times when I surely wished she'd shut up or sing something else."

"It's a haunting melody," Ellie commented, remembering the night, sitting on the front steps, when she'd heard a woman singing. And the words she'd heard had been from that song.

"I guess Mandy sang it so much because it reminded her of her baby brother, William, who died. What's wrong, Ellie? You look kinda pale all of a sudden."

"It's just that I was so surprised when I heard you singing that song." Ellie managed to sound casual. "Twice since I've lived here, I've heard someone singing it in the middle of the night."

Jake peered at her curiously. "Is that a fact? Who was it?"

Ellie shrugged. "I don't know. It sounded far away. I thought perhaps it was Priscilla Gunter. You told me, Pearl, that she sometimes wanders away from her house at night."

"Maybe." Pearl looked very doubtful. "Or maybe you just heard the wind. I know how it is when you can't sleep. Sounds seem louder and different some-how, and everything seems worse than it does by daylight."

Like last night, Ellie thought, when for a few moments she had doubted her own sanity. She shook her head. "No, it couldn't have been the wind, Pearl, because I'd never heard that song before I came here. And when I heard you singing it just now, I recognized some of the words."

"Well, then, it probably was Priscilla," Pearl said.

But Ellie could tell she doubted that explanation. Maybe Pearl thought Ellie had heard a ghost and didn't want to frighten Ellie by mentioning it. Or maybe Pearl thought that living alone in the isolated mill house was working on Ellie's nerves. She was glad she hadn't told the Vinings about the paddle wheel coming on in the middle of the night.

Ellie glanced away from Pearl's inquisitive eyes. "I'll be going to town later on, so I'd better get the mail sorted."

The Mexican restaurant where Ellie and Liz had lunch was full of tourists. They waited ten minutes for a table, which fortunately turned out to be in a corner somewhat removed from the other diners.

"We're lucky to get this table," Ellie said.

"I eat here often," Liz told her. "They all know I want this table if it's available when there's a crowd. I don't even have to ask anymore."

After they had ordered enchiladas and guacamole salad, Ellie said, "I'm glad you asked me to lunch. I needed to talk to somebody."

"I thought something was troubling you," Liz said. "I'm a good listener, and I can keep my mouth shut when it's necessary."

"Oh, it isn't any big secret. I'm just a little edgy lately."

Liz squeezed her hand sympathetically. "Ben thinks you shouldn't be living out there alone."

"I know." Ellie sighed. "And it makes me angry. I want to live there, and I'd be perfectly fine if these weird things didn't keep happening."

"Weird things?"

"Promise you won't laugh."

Liz said gravely, "Promise."

Ellie told her about the scrapings on the mill house foundation, the singing, and the paddle wheel going on seemingly spontaneously. It felt good to tell somebody. "You don't think I'm crazy, do you?"

"Of course I don't," Liz said, and she sounded as though she meant it.

"I know there are logical explanations for everything," Ellie went on. "It was probably a rat or an even larger animal that did the damage to the foundation, and the singing could have come from a passing car's radio. Or it could have been old Priscilla Gunter. But for the life of me, I can't figure out how the paddle wheel got turned on."

The waitress brought their meal, and when they were alone again, Liz said, "Ellie, would you like to sleep at my place for a while—until you're more accustomed to the isolation out there?"

"No." Ellie shook her head emphatically. She recalled her satisfaction at having the courage to go downstairs and investigate when the mill wheel came on. Slowly she was building the inner strength she wanted so much; staying with Liz would be a regression. "I want to get over these attacks of nerves as soon as possible. I have to. I don't want to give up the mill house, Liz. I haven't any place else to go."

"Not true. You have my place."

Ellie didn't want Liz to feel sorry for her. "I'll remember that. Now, tell me what you've been doing— besides working."

Liz smiled, as if Ellie's words had brought back a particularly pleasant memory. "I've been out with an old high school classmate, Hank Rushmore, twice since I saw you. He's in town for the class reunion and to visit his folks."

The name sounded vaguely familiar to Ellie. "I've heard that name somewhere . . ."

"You were with me that day at the café when Ben and I talked about him. We used to call him Tubby. He was a fat little boy, and he kept his baby fat through high school. He was a late developer. He was the shortest boy in the class when we graduated. My friends teased me because Hank had a crush on me all through school. I used to think of him as this obnoxious little twerp who embarrassed me by making cow's eyes at me all the time. Now he's six feet tall and there isn't an ounce of fat on him."

Ellie laughed. "Isn't it amazing how a few years can change things?"

"Honestly," Liz said with a chuckle, "I didn't recognize him when he came to pick me up for dinner the first time. He built a tremendously successful electronics company in Wichita. Now he's looking for another town where he can open a similar business. He's become so good-looking and self-assured. I'll be sitting there listening to him talk about going to London on business, and I'll think, 'This is Tubby Rushmore talking, Liz.' It just blows my mind."

"Apparently," Ellie teased, "he never got over his crush on you."

"Oh, that's silly," Liz protested. It was the first time Ellie had ever seen her flustered, and it amused Ellie. "I mean the man could have anybody he wanted. What could he possibly see in me? No, he's just passing a little time while he's in town. It has occurred to me that he might be toying with me—you know, making sure I realize what I missed by not taking him seriously. Not that he seems to be bragging or anything like that. Oh, I don't know, Ellie. There was never anything mysterious about Tubby in high school, but now he's somebody else. I can't begin to fathom what he's thinking half the time. It drives me crazy."

Ellie cupped her chin in her hand and listened while Liz talked. She doubted that Liz knew it yet, but she was on the verge of falling in love. Ellie hoped Hank Rushmore didn't hurt her.

A few evenings later, as Ellie sat on her front steps in the deepening dusk, she remembered her conversation with Liz and wondered if she should warn her that she had all the symptoms of a woman falling in love. But maybe Liz knew it already and was willing to risk getting hurt. Liz hadn't been through a disastrous marriage and divorce, unlike Ellie, who'd had enough of risks and emotional highs and lows. It was better to be alone. She didn't envy Liz, who was with Hank Rushmore right then—the class reunion had started at five o'clock.

Soft light from the mill house fell over a portion of the wide steps, but Ellie sat in a corner that the light couldn't reach. Wrapping her arms around herself, she leaned back against the railing. The evening was growing chilly, but she couldn't stir herself to go inside for a wrap. She didn't want to move. She just wanted to sit there and soak up the peaceful air.

She resented the intrusion when she heard a car approaching. She hoped it wasn't a carload of tourists expecting the mill to be open for business.

The car stopped beside the mill house and the headlights went off. Ben got out and walked toward her.

"Aren't you cold?"

She began to tremble, but it wasn't entirely from the cold. The light from the mill house shone on his face, highlighting angles and lines. He wore a brown suit, the jacket open over a white shirt and dark tie.

"No." Her answer issued past lips that felt stiff. She couldn't think of anything but her visit to Ben's house and the sudden passion that had sprung up between them. This was the first time she'd seen him since.

Ben moved to the steps and laid his hand on her arm. "You *are* cold. You're shaking." He sat down beside her, stripped off his jacket and slipped it over her shoulders.

"I can get a sweater—"

He pulled the jacket lapels together under her chin. "You don't need it now."

He was too close. Ellie's heart seemed to swell painfully, then settle into a too-rapid beat. "Why aren't you at the class reunion?"

"I was. I stayed through dinner and left soon after the dancing started."

She would've moved away from him, but the railing hard against her back stopped her. "Don't you like to dance, Sheriff?"

Ben leaned back, his elbows propped on the step above them, and Ellie could breathe again because he was no longer touching her. But he was still very close. "Only with the right partner," he said. "I danced a couple of times and tried to make conversation with women I hadn't seen in fifteen years. It wasn't easy."

"Did you see Liz and Hank Rushmore?"

He chuckled. "Oh, yes. Old Tubby caused quite a stir, driving up in his Porsche with Liz. He wasn't letting anybody cut in on them on the dance floor. They both seemed to be having the time of their lives."

"That's nice," Ellie murmured.

"I talked to Liz for a few minutes before dinner." He turned toward her, still leaning on one elbow. "She says you're pretty unsettled by what's been going on around here."

Ellie looked at him sharply from the shadows. "Do you still think I dreamed it all?"

"I never said that."

"You insinuated it."

He regarded her in silence for a long moment. "What

about the singing, Ellie? Why didn't you tell me about that?"

She looked away from him. "Because I knew you'd think I'd imagined it."

"That isn't true."

"Well, I didn't imagine it, Ben. I know what I heard, and I heard a woman singing a song that Pearl says Mandy Hilderbrand used to sing all the time."

His hand cupped her shoulder, and he turned her toward him, forcing her to look at him. "So, does that make it sinister—because you heard a song Mandy used to sing?"

She shivered suddenly. "No, of course not. If you don't mind, Ben, I'd rather not talk about it."

His hand remained on her shoulder and the silence thrummed between them. Finally Ben said quietly, "Hilderbrand came into my office today and gave his statement. He insists that Mandy's death was an accident."

"You don't believe him?"

His hand moved on her shoulder, massaging idly as though his mind wasn't on what he was doing. "He's hiding something. I can't prove it, but I felt it strongly after questioning him. For one thing he couldn't meet my eyes when we talked about Mandy."

"Maybe he can't accept that she wanted to end her life. They'd only been married a short while. If he admitted it, he'd probably feel it was somehow his fault. That's it, isn't it, Ben? You think Mandy committed suicide?"

He hesitated before answering. Then, "It's possible.

The other possibility is—" He halted abruptly. "I'm sorry. I shouldn't be talking to you about this."

But she knew what he'd almost said, and the knowing sent an ice-cold chill through her. "Murder? You think Oliver Hilderbrand pushed Mandy into the creek?"

"I told you I don't have anything but a feeling that Hilderbrand is hiding something."

Ellie was shaking in earnest now. "Oh, no, Ben . . ."

He pulled her against him, his arms going around her. Ellie's arms were pinned between their bodies and a flash of panic spiraled through her.

"What are you—"

"Let me warm you." He kept her close, and his hands rubbed over her back, bringing her blood rushing to heat her skin through the jacket and her shirt. He pushed his face into her hair, inhaling its sweet fragrance. "When I was dancing with those women tonight, I kept wishing it was you in my arms."

Ellie made no effort to pull away. "This is crazy." The words were muffled against his shoulder, the tone hoarse with awakened passion.

"Possibly," he agreed, his lips brushing lightly against her temple. "I tried to tell myself that my memories of the other night were exaggerated, but I haven't stopped thinking about it and wishing I hadn't let you leave when you did."

Ellie could think of no adequate reply. Her own memories of her response to Ben were too disturbing. Finally, when too much time had passed for the words to have much force, she managed, "You couldn't have stopped me."

He lifted his head and his grin flashed white. "That kiss scare you?"

"Listen, Ben—"

"It kind of stunned me, too," he interrupted. "Most of the time you seem so composed, but there wasn't any composure in that kiss."

Ellie let out a frustrated breath. "I wish you would stop talking about it. It makes me—"

"Want it to happen again?" he finished smoothly. Clearly she was trying not to let it happen, but he could feel the resistance in her body melting. He liked feeling her body against his.

"That's ridiculous." Ellie was trapped by his warmth, her body softening in betrayal.

"Is it?" Ben pulled her closer. His eyes held hers. His warm breath skimmed across her cheek. "I'm going to do it again, and we'll see."

Ellie's eyes widened. Why was he doing this to her? Why couldn't he have just driven on past tonight? "I don't think that's a smart idea," she whispered. "Not at all."

One corner of his mouth lifted in wry acknowledgment, but he didn't relax his hold on her. "Oh, Ellie," he said, his voice amused and husky, "who said anything about smart? This was ordained the minute I got here tonight. We can't fight fate."

"Fate! Ben, I've heard a line or two before—"

She found herself cut off as he took her mouth. The remainder of her protest was trapped in her throat as his tongue slowly entered her mouth to coax and seduce. What remained of her weak resistance melted instantly. Ben knew the final impediment of her will had given way when her arms wrapped themselves around his neck. Just as it had the first time he'd kissed her, Ben's desire was unleashed instantly, throbbing wildly through his body.

Ellie's mouth moved under his, opening for him, actively seeking more. Rational thought was a thing from another life. Her mind churned with pure wanting, her body came alive with sensations she hadn't known before, or had forgotten long ago. His mobile lips and the seduction of his tongue ignited a fire of need inside her. She could feel the same need in him, and it thrilled her.

Never in her life before had she so abandoned herself to feeling. She desperately needed to be touched by him. Everywhere. The ache for it was almost painful. She murmured his name, but the sound that came from her throat had lost coherence.

Feeling her response was like a shock of electricity to Ben. He wanted her. Crazy, she'd said. Maybe she wasn't so far wrong, after all. His need for her was a fever of madness. He'd never felt anything approaching it before.

He wrenched his mouth from hers, gulping air. "I want you, Ellie. Let me take you inside."

Her breathing was almost as unsteady as his. She felt as though she had been awakened abruptly from a dream. For an instant, she wondered where she was, who she was. She stared into Ben's desire-glazed eyes and her brain began to clear. "That's impossible." She barely recognized the whispery voice as her own. Her body burned with thwarted passion.

"What's to stop us?" He drew her back for a brief,

demanding kiss. Shaken by her heedless response to him, Ellie pulled out of his arms. Her knees shook as she got up and she steadied herself by gripping the railing.

She took a deep breath. "I don't know how I could have forgotten myself like that." She handed him his jacket, trying to sound calm and reasonable. "Obviously, the isolation is getting to me more than I realized." She took another quick breath. "I don't know what your excuse is, Ben, but I think the best thing for both of us is to forget what just happened."

Silently, he got to his feet, tossing his jacket over his shoulder. He smiled down at her, an odd, pensive smile. "Do you really think we can do that, Ellie?"

"Yes, I do," she stated emphatically. She let go of the railing, found her legs would support her, and strode to the mill house door. She turned to look back at him. "Good night." Then she stepped inside and shut the door firmly behind her.

Chapter Eight

Ellie was thinking about getting up the next morning at seven-thirty when the telephone beside her bed shrilled. She sat up and reached for it.

"Hello."

"Morning, Ellie."

"Ben?" She sighed and lay back.

"I didn't sleep well, did you?"

"I slept like a log," she lied. "What do you want?"

"You left yourself wide open with that one. Do you really want me to tell you what I want?"

An irrepressible smile lit her face, and she was thankful he couldn't see it. She'd given him too much encouragement already. "Don't be cute, Ben." She heard him chuckle.

"It's called flirting."

A bubble of laughter escaped her. She was reminded of her high school days when her boyfriend had called to say good night. It had felt deliciously wicked to be lying in bed, engaging in risqué conversation that they would never have dared face to face. But Ben Stapleton was no shy sixteen-year-old. "Aren't you going to be late for work, Sheriff?"

"I've been thinking about that singing you heard," he said, ignoring her question. "Maybe somebody's trying to get you out of the mill by making you think Mandy's ghost is haunting it."

"I don't believe in ghosts."

"No," he said slowly, considering. "But nobody is completely immune to eerie, unexplainable happenings."

"Are you trying to scare me, Sheriff? Because if you are, you can save your breath."

"Good. Actually, I called about Thursday night."

"What about it?"

"I'd like to take you to dinner."

"Where?" she asked suspiciously. She had better sense than to go to Ben's house again.

"In Fayetteville."

"Ben," she began, "I don't want to go out with you."

"You can't spend all your time at the mill, Ellie. I'm worried about you."

"Do me a favor, and don't worry about me." Relaxed, she stretched and snuggled down into the pillows.

"I'm the sheriff of this county. It's my job."

"Are you sure?" she asked lightly.

"Absolutely. You'll be perfectly safe with me in Fayetteville."

Ellie groaned inwardly, thinking that Ben was the last person she'd feel safe with. "Ben, I don't think—"

"I'll pick you up at six."

"I haven't said I'd go. Do you have a hearing problem?"

"Six, Thursday," he repeated. "It's an hour's drive."

Feeling sleepy again, she yawned and tried to remember why she shouldn't go out with Ben. What harm would it do to go to Fayetteville with him? "I'll think about it."

"See you Thursday, Ellie."

She was smiling as she hung up. She was tempted to let herself drift back into sleep, but it was seven-forty. The Vinings would be there in twenty minutes. Grumbling, she tossed back the covers and got ready for the day.

Jake arrived carrying an animal skin, which he proudly displayed for Ellie's inspection.

"What is it?" she asked.

Pearl and Jake laughed at her ignorance. "It's a coyote skin, gal," Jake said. "I found him in one of my traps last week. This is a near-perfect pelt. It'll bring a good price."

Ellie's mind got caught on the word "traps," and she had a mental picture of the animal struggling and struggling to get away. Paling, she said, "That's nice, Jake, but would you mind leaving that in the truck?"

"You're upsetting her, Jake," Pearl said.

"Aw, Ellie," Jake said, "don't waste your sympathy

on that coyote. Comin' from the city like you do, you ain't got no idea what a nuisance coyotes are. They destroyed my watermelon crop last year. Why, it was probably coyotes that killed the Swafford boy."

"I understand," murmured Ellie, "but it doesn't make me feel any better about this coyote."

Jake looked offended. "Ain't you the gal that bought a sackful of rat poison the other day? I can't see no difference between spreading around rat poison and trapping coyotes."

Ellie shrugged, laughing at herself. "There probably isn't any difference," she admitted. "In fact, I haven't been able to bring myself to put out the poison. I was hoping you'd do it for me, Jake."

He shook his head. "I'll do it this morning. You're too soft-hearted for your own good, Ellie. Now, about this pelt, what if I spread it over the railing out front just for today so folks could see it?"

"Fine, Jake," Ellie relented. At least she wouldn't have to look at it all day.

Ellie sorted the mail, then helped Pearl and Jake mix and sack several kinds of quick mixes.

"I wonder if the reverend ever went to town to answer the sheriff's questions," Jake mused. He was taping the openings of the sacks as Ellie and Pearl finished with them.

"Yes," Ellie said. "Ben told me Mr. Hilderbrand had been in to see him."

"Maybe Ben'll let the thing drop now," Pearl speculated.

"I'm not so sure he will," Ellie said. "Ben seems to think that Hilderbrand isn't telling all he knows. He thinks Mandy might have killed herself." She wouldn't tell them that Ben hadn't ruled out the possibility of murder. Ellie refused to believe that the mild-mannered Oliver Hilderbrand was a killer, and the less said about it the better.

"I'll never believe that," Jake said. "Mandy just wasn't the type. Anyway, she musta been happy with the reverend. He pampered her like you wouldn't believe, let her come and go just as she pleased. Never asked her to do any of the work around here, even cooked their meals himself."

"Now, Jake, you never could tell what Mandy was thinking," Pearl put in. "Ben may have something there. I was telling my neighbor about that singing you been hearing, Ellie. She says Mandy's ghost is haunting this mill, that there musta been something fishy about her death to make her come back. Now if she committed suicide—"

"But I thought you said ghosts come back only when they've been murdered."

"Not necessarily. I once heard about a woman that killed herself and came back to haunt her husband because he didn't bury her in the churchyard. Finally, he moved her casket over to the church, and she never bothered him again."

Jake shot Ellie an eloquent look. "Did I ever tell you about the ghost I saw one time, Ellie?"

He was grinning, so Ellie knew he wasn't serious. He was trying to take her mind off Pearl's talk about Mandy's ghost. "No."

"Well, 'bout two miles the other side of Springville, there's a bend in the road where a man was killed when

I was a young man. He was thrown outa his car onto a big white rock by the side of the road. Folks began telling that his blood wouldn't wash off that rock, and people got scared to pass by there. Some of 'em claimed somethin' got on behind their mules and horses and rode with 'em and spooked their animals. I was a'courtin' up there and I had to come by that rock. To make it worse, it was raining that night and I didn't know whether to believe those ghost tales or not. I was a'horseback, and when I started around that bend, my horse got scared and bowed up and wouldn't budge an inch. I could feel him shakin'. And 'bout that time I saw somethin' white coming out from behind that rock." Jake cackled at Ellie's smiling, earnest attention. "I thought I was a goner, for sure. Well, my horse figured out what that thing was before I did. He stopped shakin' and started walking around the bend as nice as you please. I got a match outa my coat pocket and struck it, and there set a big white shepherd dog. Now, if I'd gone on without striking that match, I'd be saying to this day that I'd seen a ghost."

Jake slapped his leg and cackled, and Ellie laughed with him. Pearl went on making corn muffin mix. "That don't make all ghost stories lies," she said.

"I never said they was outright lies," Jake told her. "A lot of folks probably believe they've seen a ghost, but it's because they let their imagination work on a thing until they think it's real."

Ellie would have liked to agree with Jake, but she didn't want to hurt Pearl's feelings. So she began to talk about the best way to ship the mill's orders.

Several times during the day, whenever she was

alone, Ellie's mind drifted back to Ben's phone call that morning. Was she going to dinner with Ben on Thursday? She had to decide soon and let him know if she wasn't. But she didn't have to make up her mind today, she told herself.

Ben spent most of the day in his office at the courthouse, catching up on paperwork. Like Ellie, he found his mind returning again and again to the morning's telephone conversation—and the previous evening when Ellie had melted in his arms before running away.

Ben was troubled. How much did he really know about Ellie? His first impressions had all been negative, and in his work he'd learned to heed first impressions. They were right more often than they were wrong.

If he were a betting man, he'd have bet that operating the mill was nothing but a whim. Bored women who didn't have enough to occupy their time had passing fancies, he'd noticed. They were always into something new—belly dancing or making paper flowers or whatever. He'd 've bet that Ellie'd received a juicy settlement from that doctor husband of hers and didn't need to work at all. He'd given her two weeks to come to her senses and move on.

But it would soon be a month since Ellie moved into the mill, and as far as he could tell she wasn't thinking of leaving. Even with the strange goings-on out there. Unaccountably, it made him feel like a traitor to doubt her; but he still wondered now and then if all of those things had actually happened exactly the way Ellie told it. Oh, he thought she believed it, but there had to be a logical explanation. She must have accidentally left the mill open the night the paddle wheel was turned on by somebody—Jimmy Gunter was still the most likely suspect on Ben's list. That was just the kind of thing a kid would get a kick out of. Priscilla Gunter could have been the singer Ellie heard, and he'd always believed those other noises had been made by mice.

But he could tell that Ellie was disturbed by the occurrences. If occurrences they were—there was always the possibility that Ellie had imagined everything. Ben had been more inclined to that explanation in the beginning, but the more he saw of Ellie, the less he was satisfied with it.

There was more substance to Eleanor Harper than he had thought at first. Once or twice she'd forgotten to be the woman she presented to the world, and Ben had seen flashes of vulnerability. Whatever had happened in Houston had been painful for her and she was still marked by it, even though she succeeded in hiding it most of the time. At their first meeting, he hadn't suspected the passion that lay beneath her surface, for she hid that very well, too. But he had touched that passion, twice now, and it had left him hungry to know Ellie better. He was becoming more attracted to her all the time. That troubled him. What if his first impression of her had been correct? Worse, what if *he* was just another passing fancy?

Ben ran both hands through his hair and came out of his reverie. The pile of morning mail still lay on his desk, unopened. He reached for a letter opener and began slitting the envelopes.

The third envelope contained a wallet-sized photograph of a young girl. He read the accompanying letter. It was from Warren Brohaugh, the Tulsa man who had come to his office several weeks ago in his search for his runaway daughter. Anne Brohaugh still hadn't come home, the letter said. Brohaugh gave Anne's physical description—5 feet 3, 100 pounds, blond hair, blue eyes, age sixteen, last seen wearing blue jeans, red knit shirt, and brown sandals.

Ben looked at the pretty, laughing girl in the photograph and wondered what had gone wrong between her and her parents. She had been gone too long; it didn't look good.

He carried the letter and photograph out to the deputy on duty. "Let's get this on the wire," he said. "This kid may be in real trouble. Her parents haven't heard from her in two months."

Back at his desk, he went through the file on Jimmy Gunter and the Crowder brothers. He had an appointment with the D. A. and the public defender next week to discuss the case. If those dumb kids would only tell what they'd done with the stolen items, there would be no problem in getting them probation. He made a note to talk to the boys again about that before his meeting with the D. A. and the boys' attorney. While he was at it, he'd ask Jimmy if he'd happened by the mill one night, found it open, and turned on the paddle wheel.

"Gonna rain before morning." Jake sniffed the air as he and Pearl left the mill for the day.

Ellie had followed them to the front door and watched Jake carefully folding his coyote pelt to take home with him. She went down the front steps as the

Vinings got into their pickup. "See you in the morning."

"If the road's not washed out," Jake replied.

"Does that happen often?" Ellie queried, worried.

Pearl started the truck's mufflerless engine. "Only when we have a real gully washer," she called over the noise. "The lane from the county road to our cabin ain't graveled."

"Gonna get that done one of these days," Jake hollered as the pickup jolted away.

Ellie watched the truck until it was lost to sight. Then she lifted her face to the sky. The black clouds that had been far to the west that morning hung overhead, blotting out the sun.

Her gaze shifted to the mill house. The second-floor windows were black and empty. Frail light spilled gloomily from the open front door over the steps, turning them a grayish-white. Behind the mill, the sky was the color of gun metal. The colorful foliage of the surrounding trees had been grayed out, and the woods seemed too close and oppressive. Ellie felt a tingle at the back of her scalp. To her puzzlement, she was reluctant to go back inside.

"Ellie, you're being silly," she chided herself aloud. The sound of her voice was frail in the windless silence. Shaking off the feeling of gloom, she walked back into the mill house.

She had very little business during the remainder of the afternoon. The threatened rain kept people in town. When she went up to her apartment at five, she felt restless and vigorously attacked the four rooms with vacuum and dust cloth until they shone. For the first time, the bare windows bothered her, and it didn't help much to tell herself that there was nobody within a half mile to look in at her. She made her dinner, and the heat from the range turned the apartment too warm and stuffy. She opened two windows at opposite ends of the apartment to let the cool night air drift through.

She lay in bed for some time before she was able to sleep. The storm awakened her. When the rain came, it wasn't a gentle autumn shower like the ones they'd had during the past month. It began as a gushing downpour that battered against the roof and windows, punctuated by explosions of thunder and crackling flashes of lightning.

The first clap of thunder jerked Ellie upright in bed. A jagged shaft of lightning speared through the gloom, lighting the bedroom momentarily, and was followed by another rumble of thunder that echoed loudly in the darkness.

Ellie fumbled for the bedside lamp and switched it on, but the darkness remained. Grumbling, she crawled from the bed and felt her way to the wall light switch. But the ceiling light didn't come on either. The storm had knocked out the electricity.

Cursing beneath her breath, Ellie felt her way into the living room and stood in a puddle of water to shut the window, then slowly made her way to the kitchen where she'd left a second window open over the sink. The windowsill was drenched with rain. She slammed the window shut and grabbed the towel that hung next to the sink to dry the sill.

Lightning flashed and, for the briefest moment through the pelting rain, the old bridge behind the mill house was revealed in every detail. In that moment Ellie saw something moving on the bridge—the figure of a woman in a white gown.

She froze, her hand holding the towel on the windowsill, waiting for the lightning to flash again. The rain whipped against the window, and the wind that had built while she slept was one continuous moan.

She began to tremble with fear. Her heart thudded wildly. Had she really seen a woman on the bridge? It couldn't be. No woman in her right mind would be walking around in this storm. In her right mind . . . If her neighbors could be believed, Priscilla Gunter wasn't in her right mind. But the woman had moved, in the brief glimpse Ellie had had of her, with the easy grace of youth.

Her dress had been white, reaching almost to her feet. Jake had said that Mandy Hilderbrand wore white frequently. And Pearl and her friends believed that Mandy's ghost was haunting the mill, because there was "something fishy" about the way she died.

Murder? Was Ben right about that? Was Mandy murdered?

Ellie was shaking in earnest now. She took several deep breaths and told herself she was acting like a child, scaring herself with ghost stories.

"Good Lord, Ellie, your Houston set wouldn't believe it!" The sound of her voice seemed to lessen the tension. She even managed a weak laugh at herself. But more and more her nine years in Houston seemed to have been a part of somebody else's life.

As she was hanging the towel back on its rack, the lightning speared the darkness again. Ellie's gaze sped from one end of the bridge to the other. No one was there.

She felt her way back to bed. Rain had dampened the front of her gown and she was shivering. She stripped the gown off before crawling between the covers and pulling them up to her chin.

She remembered Jake's reminiscing that day and told herself dryly that maybe what she'd seen was a big, white dog.

No. She hadn't seen anything but the bridge. She'd been looking through pouring rain and the flash of lightning had lasted but an instant. There hadn't been time to see anything clearly.

"You're losing your grip, old girl," she muttered. She wouldn't allow her imagination these flights of fancy. She couldn't allow it. She might have been through a difficult time, but she was an intelligent woman and as sane as anybody.

She curled her body into a ball until warmth surrounded her. Eventually, the storm still raging outside, she fell asleep.

Chapter Nine

"Good morning, Oliver."

Hilderbrand hadn't come into the mill for a few days, and he looked pale.

"Morning, Ellie."

"I've missed seeing you lately. Have you been ill?"

"Just a cold." For a moment he watched the Vinings working over the bins. Then he sorted through the mail in his box, saw it was all advertising material, and tossed it into Ellie's trash can. "I'll go say hello to Pearl and Jake."

Ellie watched his spare figure shuffle toward the back and thought that he seemed to have aged since the last time she saw him.

Hilderbrand chatted with the Vinings and helped

them with their work for over an hour while Ellie was busy in the post office. When she had a breather, she invited Hilderbrand to have tea with her.

He seemed glad to accept, and they sat at the oak table. "Oliver," Ellie said, stirring a spoonful of honey into her tea, "are you all right?"

His dark eyes darted to her face and for a moment he looked frightened. He glanced away. "I'm fine, Ellie. Why wouldn't I be?"

"You don't look well. Shouldn't you have a telephone put in at your cabin? What if you needed a doctor?"

"Can't afford it," he responded, as though he was embarrassed to admit it. "I don't really want a phone, anyway. Devilish instrument." He blew on his tea before sipping it.

Ellie chuckled. "Maybe so, but I couldn't do without one here."

"How's business?" Hilderbrand asked, and Ellie caught an edge of regret in his tone. He really missed the mill, but evidently he couldn't bring himself to live there after Mandy's death.

"Good. You miss it, don't you, Oliver?"

He shrugged. "Sometimes. I worked so hard on the mill. You can't appreciate it unless you'd seen the state it was in when I found it. That whole north wall had slipped off the foundation. Had to rebuild it completely. And the roof leaked like a sieve. Yes, I miss it, but don't worry, Ellie. I have every intention of honoring our agreement. I couldn't ever live here again, after what happened."

Ellie's expression softened sympathetically. "The Vinings told me how Mandy died. I'm so sorry, Oliver. I know you must miss her terribly."

He drew a deep breath. "Oh, yes. Mandy's—well, I never knew anyone else like her. I was awfully disillusioned when I came here. With my congregation, religion, life in general. It seemed that everybody had an angle, an ax to grind. Even so-called Christians. I began to question the validity of organized religion. When a member of my congregation had a serious problem, religion didn't seem to help much. The words of comfort I tried to offer sounded hollow. Finally, I resigned my ministry."

Ellie sensed that he was speaking from the depths of his heart, and she didn't know what to say except to repeat, "I'm sorry."

"I came here with everything I owned in a pack on my back. Camped in the woods about a mile from here. Mandy watched me for days before she would show herself openly. I knew she was there, for I caught a glimpse of her now and then, but I pretended not to know. Then she got to where she came to see me every day, usually for lunch." He smiled sadly, as if remembering a particularly poignant scene. "I was enthralled. She seemed to be the perfect example of what the human race would be without civilization. Natural, unspoiled, free."

"I wish I could've known her," Ellie murmured.

He drank from his teacup, his eyes narrowed reflectively. "Knowing Mandy deepened my doubts about the existence of God."

Ellie waited for him to explain, but he seemed lost in some private memory. "I don't understand."

His eyes lost their vague expression and focused once more on Ellie. "She was a natural creature—half-wild really—and she was completely amoral. Had no sense of right and wrong. Yet all religions teach that human beings are born with that sense. 'A sense of ought,' some theologians call it. Religions cite it as evidence of a higher power."

He sounded so disillusioned that it made Ellie feel like crying. "That isn't very scientific research," she said gently. "I mean, you had no one but Mandy to judge by."

He looked at her sharply and laughed. It wasn't an amused laugh, but more surprised, as though her argument had been unexpected. "You're right, of course. After we were married, I began to suspect that Mandy was unique, maybe even a little crazy. But I loved her. I wanted to take care of her for the rest of my life." He sounded more like a doting father than a husband. He looked at the callused hand gripping his teacup. "The sheriff thinks Mandy took her own life."

"Did he tell you that?" Ellie's tone was noncommittal.

"Not in so many words. But he kept making me go back over that morning when Mandy died, again and again, as if he thought I was leaving out something—did Mandy and I argue that morning, had she been unhappy."

"Could she have committed suicide?" Ellie asked quietly.

He looked at her a long moment before answering. "I don't want to think she could do that," he said simply.

He desperately wanted to believe he'd made Mandy happy, Ellie saw. But the bleakness in his eyes told her he hadn't been able to convince himself completely. Nor was he certain that Mandy hadn't been capable of killing herself. Suddenly she remembered Jake's account of Mandy's death. Upon learning of it, Hilderbrand's first words had been, *Mandy, Mandy, what have you done?*

He shuffled his feet and pushed his chair back. "I think I'll walk over to the Gunters before I go home. Jimmy helped me some when I was restoring the mill and we got to be pretty good friends. I'm trying to convince him to make a clean breast of things, turn the loot from the high school robbery over to the sheriff, or, if they no longer have it, tell what they did with it. I'm afraid the Crowder boys have threatened to beat him up if he tells. But I've got him thinking about it, anyway. That boy needs a friend, and I like to think our talks have been good for him."

Ellie suspected the conversations with Jimmy Gunter had helped Oliver as much as Jimmy. He was terribly lonely. "It's kind of you to think of Jimmy when your own loss is so recent."

He shrugged this away. "Counseling was an important part of my ministry. I can't stop being a preacher altogether, I guess. Are you going to make deliveries tomorrow? I can leave the van with you now."

Ellie had continued to vacillate over whether to go to Fayetteville with Ben the next day. But there was a pile of orders ready to be delivered. It was a perfect excuse to turn Ben down. *Coward,* an inner voice whispered. But she ignored it and said, "Thank you, Oliver. I would like to make deliveries in person one more time. You can take my car—"

He waved her suggestion aside. "No, no. I prefer walking. When will you be back?"

"Friday evening."

"Fine. I'll come for the van on Saturday."

Ellie spent the rest of the day trying to gather the courage to call Ben and tell him she would be gone Thursday. Why did the idea of calling him make her so uneasy? Was she afraid he'd talk her out of going? Afraid that, deep down, she wanted to be talked out of it?

She finally took the cowardly way out and left a note for Ben taped to the front door of the mill house. After all, she told herself, she had never really accepted his invitation. She'd only said she'd think about it.

It was dark when Ellie returned Friday evening. She had succeeded in keeping her mind occupied with business until the last hundred miles when she had begun to wonder about Ben's reaction to her note. Was he furious with her?

Sometime during the past hour, she had admitted to herself that he had a right to be furious. It had been really chicken of her not to have told him in person that she was going away. She would have to apologize to him when she saw him. But what if he was so angry he wouldn't accept her apology?

That didn't bear thinking on.

She gathered her overnight bag, purse, and packages containing some things she had bought for the apartment and let herself into the mill house. The Vinings hadn't left a light on, and she fumbled in the dark for several moments before finding the switch next to the front door.

Light flooded the ground floor. Ellie glanced around quickly. Some instinct had alerted her senses. She had the feeling that someone had been there not long ago. But there was no one there now.

Perhaps the Vinings had worked late, she told herself. Trying to shake off the feeling, she climbed the stairs.

She dropped her packages just inside the apartment door and, flipping on lights as she walked, went directly to the bathroom with her overnight case. She needed a hot bath and, after that, something to eat.

She poured bubble bath into the running water and pinned her hair up off her neck before climbing in. Sighing, she sank beneath the bubbles, feeling the exquisite pleasure of her muscles relaxing, one by one, as the hot water caressed her skin.

Running a washcloth over her face, she tried to remember what she had in the refrigerator for dinner. Cottage cheese. Leftover roast beef. She wrinkled her nose. Not very appetizing. She should have stopped in Springville for something to eat, but she'd been tired and eager to get home.

Bacon and eggs. Hot biscuits. That sounded much better. Her stomach grumbled hungrily as she envisioned a biscuit piled with melting butter and strawberry jam.

She finished her bath hastily, brushed her teeth, donned robe and scuffs, and headed through her bedroom toward the kitchen. But something about her bed made her turn back at the door for a better look. There was a faint hump in the middle of the bed, as though a small pillow had been left between the sheets when it was made. But it couldn't be a pillow. She'd made the bed herself Thursday morning. Had she been in such a hurry to be gone that she'd left the sheets bunched up in the middle?

The instinct that had made her uneasy upon her entry downstairs had deserted her completely. She had no forewarning, no sense of danger. She felt merely curious as she walked to the bed and turned back the spread and top sheet.

A rattlesnake lay coiled in the center of her bed. As she stripped the covers back, it lifted its evil-looking head and hissed at her.

Ellie recoiled. Terror speared through her like a huge, vicious knife. While it was happening, it seemed that several minutes passed as she stood there, paralyzed, and watched the snake slithering into tighter coils, preparing to strike. But later she realized it could only have been a second or two before the panicked paralysis released her and she bolted for the door.

She ran for the living room, scattering the packages she'd left near the front door, and reached the landing, slamming the door shut behind her. But irrationally an ordinary wood door between her and the snake didn't seem enough. She tore down the stairs, taking them two at a time and losing her scuffs as she went, desperate to put more space between herself and the rattler.

She dashed behind the post office counter, grabbed the telephone receiver off its hook, and without hesitation, dialed Ben's number. It didn't occur to her until after she'd hung up to wonder if he might not have been alone.

"Sheriff Stapleton sp—"

She didn't wait for him to finish. "Ben! Ben, you have to come over here right away!"

"Ellie?"

"Yes! Oh, God, Ben, please hurry!"

"I take it you've returned from your big business trip." He didn't sound like a man in a hurry. In fact, he drawled the words out as though he had all the time in the world.

"We can talk about that later!"

"Sell lots of flour, did you?"

Ellie's panic and fear and anger converged on her simultaneously. She burst into tears.

"Ellie, what's wrong?" He wasn't drawling any longer.

She couldn't make sense for a moment. She'd kill him when she saw him! "It's a rattlesnake," she finally choked out. "In my bed."

"Are—" He halted and Ellie thought, *If he asks me if I'm sure, I'll kill him with my bare hands!* "Hang tight, Ellie. I'll be right there." He broke the connection.

Ellie's hand was shaking so badly it took several tries for her to fit the receiver back into its cradle. When she did, she walked cautiously to the foot of the stairs and looked up. No sign of the snake. *Be sensible, Ellie*, she scolded herself, *snakes can't open doors*.

The mere thought of the snake slithering down the stairs made her skin crawl hideously. She couldn't stand to stay in the mill house. She turned on the outside lights and, barefooted, went outside and locked herself inside her car. She pulled her knees up to her chest and her robe down over her legs to try to ward off the cold.

Ben arrived in about three minutes. He must have dressed in record time, Ellie thought gratefully as his car pulled to a stop beside hers. A pistol dangled from one hand. She rolled down her window.

"Thank you for coming."

He eyed her huddled state, her arms hugging her legs, bare toes peeking out from beneath her robe. "Do you know where the snake is now?"

She shook her head. "I shut the apartment door and left it inside."

"Wait here." He entered the mill house and she heard his boots on the stairs.

She sat, shivering, for long minutes before a single gunshot sounded and she jerked violently. A few minutes later, Ben came out of the mill house, the limp snake draped over his pistol barrel. He walked to the woods and flung the snake in. He stopped at his car to put the pistol in his glove compartment.

Ellie opened her car door slowly. Ben reached her just as her feet slid to the ground. "Wh—where did you find it?"

"Under your bed." She looked delectable in that white satin robe with wisps of auburn hair hanging around her face, having escaped the pins at the back of her head. She was shivering, and he put his hands on her arms. "Tell me what happened."

His hard palms warmed her skin. "I got home less than an hour ago. I went up to the apartment, directly to the bathroom to run a bath. I didn't notice that there was something in my bed until I came out of the bathroom. It—it was under the covers—a hump beneath the spread."

"And the front door of the mill house was locked when you arrived?" His hands were gliding gently up and down her arms until she felt her skin begin to pulse. It was an incredibly erotic sensation.

"Yes," she whispered. "I've no idea how a snake could've gotten into my bed."

"He didn't get there by himself."

"No . . . I don't suppose he did." He meant that somebody had gone into her bedroom while she was away and left the snake. But how? And who? The questions drifted to the periphery of her thoughts as she became more and more aware of Ben's hands caressing her. "Don't," she whispered, afraid she would be unable to prevent herself from melting into his arms.

"You left your house shoes on the stairs," he murmured, then casually slid his arms around her and lifted her.

"I can walk," she protested weakly, but he ignored her and strode into the mill house, kicked the door shut behind them, and climbed the stairs with Ellie held close against his chest.

He let her down in her living room, and the world

steadied again as her feet found the floor. But her knees were still trembling and she didn't take the step back that would have put a safer distance between them.

"You'll probably take cold from this," he accused, and kissed her before she could prevent it.

"I'm as healthy as a horse." Ellie was distracted by the kiss, and she turned away to say nervously, "I have to change the sheets."

Ben lounged against the door facing and watched her strip the bed. She wasn't aware that when she passed in front of the bedside lamp, the outlines of her body were revealed through the satin robe as clearly as if she wore nothing at all. He was enchanted.

"It doesn't make sense," she stated, shaking a pillow out of its case. "I haven't done anything to make somebody do such a vicious thing."

Ben tried to pull himself out of the erotic fantasy his mind was weaving. "Who knew you would be gone this evening?"

"The Vinings." She turned her back to get fresh bed linens from a bureau. "You, of course," she added with a quirk of a smile as she flipped a clean sheet over the bed.

"And Hilderbrand. You drove his van."

"Yes." Frowning, she tucked the corners around the mattress and straightened. "But then Jake and Pearl could have told dozens of people who came into the mill yesterday and today. Anybody who asked where I was."

"Hmmm."

Ben had tossed her scuffs into a corner, and she

stepped into them. "I was going to fix bacon and eggs before I was distracted." She gazed at him solemnly from across the room. "I haven't had supper. I could make enough for you."

For a moment Ben didn't move. The look in his eyes made her pulse beat too rapidly. Then he straightened, leaving room for her to pass through the doorway. "I'd like that."

Being alone with Ben in the small apartment surrounded by the Ozark night made her so anxious that her knees started to tremble again. But it seemed so easy for him, she thought. She felt his gaze on the back of her head as he followed her into the kitchen, and she had to resist an impulse to repin her straggling hair. In the kitchen she handed him a cookie sheet and a tin of biscuit dough. "You can put these in the oven while I fry the bacon."

"This is heresy."

She narrowed her eyes at his easy smile. "What do you mean?"

He tapped the tin against the corner of the cabinet. "All that natural stuff downstairs, and we're having canned biscuits?" He began to arrange the circles of dough on the cookie sheet.

Ellie laughed. She hadn't seen the humor in the situation until Ben pointed it out, and laughing made her feel easier with him. "I'm in a hurry. And if you tell, I'll deny it with my last breath." She slapped strips of bacon into a big skillet.

Ben slid the biscuits into the oven, then without being told found placemats, plates and silver and set the pine trestle table. The kitchen reminded him of Ellie. Compact and sparkling clean. Ivy and other live plants sat on windowsills and hung by sisal braids of various lengths from the ceiling. Masses of bright autumn leaves spilled from a white ironstone jug in the center of the table. It was a cozy, intimate room.

"Are you comfortable here?"

"Completely."

"It must be much smaller"—he paused, then smiled apologetically—"than you're used to."

She broke eggs into a bowl without looking at him. "I'm used to this now."

When everything was ready, she poured glasses of milk and set butter, honey, and strawberry jam on the table.

Ben watched her split a biscuit, add butter and jam, and take an appreciative bite. Her tongue flicked out to remove a trace of jam from her bottom lip, and when she looked up, she found him studying her with suppressed desire building in his eyes. And she felt her own being kindled.

Ellie tore her eyes away and helped herself to scrambled eggs. "Why did you decide to become a sheriff?"

"I didn't." He caught Ellie's questioning glance. "I was a state trooper, working out of Fayetteville. My father was sheriff of Spring County for thirty years. When he was sixty, Mom wanted him to retire and move to Florida. But he said he wouldn't unless I'd come back and take over for him. So Mom started in on me. It's hard for anybody to say no to my mother.

Anyway, before I knew what was happening, I was appointed to finish out Dad's term. That was three years ago. I was reelected a year later."

"Have you regretted it?"

"Not often." He moved his shoulders and grinned. "Only at the peak of the tourist season."

She understood what he meant. She knew that the mill couldn't operate profitably without the tourist trade, but she was already looking forward to the quiet winter months. "You have to take the bad with the good." She bit into a crisp piece of bacon. "Ummm, this is wonderful." She smiled. "Even the canned biscuits. I was starving." She sighed with pleasure as the farm-fresh eggs and bacon melted in her mouth.

It gave him pleasure to watch her eat. "I was pretty annoyed when I found that note taped to your door." Her fork slid lightly between her teeth.

"Were you? I'm sorry. I should have phoned, but I . . ." She shrugged helplessly. "I didn't have the nerve, I guess."

"Why?" he asked curiously.

"You might have talked me out of going," she stated. "And I needed to go."

"To make deliveries?" he inquired. "Or to avoid going out with me?"

Ellie sighed. "Maybe some of both." She hadn't meant to admit that and was astonished it had slipped out. "What I'm trying to say," she continued, "is that I'm not sure I can handle something like that right now."

He studied her for a moment. "Like what, a dinner date?"

"You know what I mean," she countered.

He knew exactly. Things crackled between them when they were together, but he hadn't been sure before that she'd felt it, too. It gave him a certain satisfaction to know that she had. "Were you hurt so badly?"

It was difficult to keep her eyes level and composed. "Hurt and humiliated. But more than anything, I was scared."

He realized that what she had been scared of was being on her own. She had been very young when she married. For the first time, he thought he understood her reason for taking on the mill. She wanted to prove to herself that she could handle it. He sensed he'd pushed far enough for the moment. It was something of a victory that she'd admitted that much. "Do you plan to exercise your option and buy the mill?"

Ellie looked at him for a moment. She'd been marshalling her defenses, and the change of topic disconcerted her. She felt her tense muscles relaxing again. "I don't have to decide for more than four months, but if I had to decide today, I'd say yes. I love everything about the mill except . . ." She made a vague gesture with her shoulders.

He knew that she was thinking about the snake in her bed and the other unexplained happenings. They'd get to the bottom of it, but he didn't want to tell her he'd been asking a few questions of the neighbors. He hadn't turned up anything, though, so there was really nothing to tell. And he didn't want her to worry any more tonight.

"You're lucky to have the Vinings working for you."

Ellie lifted a brow. "I couldn't have made it without them." A smile tugged at her lips. "Of course, Pearl's ghost stories go along with the job."

Ben grinned. "As you said, the bad with the good. And Pearl is a superstitious soul."

"But well meaning."

They finished off the eggs, bacon, and biscuits, and Ellie took the plates away. Ben sat back and watched her. Contentment spread through him. Having relaxed during the meal, Ellie didn't mind having him watch her. In fact, she dreaded the moment when he would have to go. She couldn't deny that she enjoyed his company. He made her feel alive. She must be careful, she warned herself, not to begin to depend on him.

She had tucked the dishes into the dishwasher and was drying her hands when he came up behind her and laid is hands on her shoulders. "This is better than going to Fayetteville," he murmured, and slowly, lightly, began to brush his lips across her cheek.

Ellie's breath stilled. She couldn't move. Her body had sprung to life under his gentle touch and she was locked in the shock of sensation. When he turned her around to face him, she was unable to speak. He wrapped his hand around the back of her neck. Her eyes were held by his, and then he lowered his head and passed his lips over hers.

He lifted his head to look deeply into her eyes again. He watched passion warring with wariness in her dark irises. "You taste good," he murmured.

Ellie shook her head, as if to dispel a powerful drug, and stepping to one side, walked away from him. She placed one hand on the wall to steady herself. She

would stop shaking in a minute. The need would pass.
Her breath caught on a gasp when Ben turned her back
into his arms.

She sighed and closed her eyes. Her body was all
yielding softness as he drew her closer. She felt dizzy
and leaned against him. When his warm breath whispered across her cheek, she sighed again and shuddered.

I have to stop him, she told herself. *I have to stop
myself.* Slowly her arms found their way around his
neck, her fingers threaded through his hair. *I must be
crazy not to stop this right now.* His body settled hard
against her, and a shimmering warmth was building in
her. His hands slid up her back and down again to rest
on the curve of her hips. When his lips brushed her
earlobe and pressed into her neck, she made a soft
sound of pleasure deep in her throat.

"I'm not ready for this," she murmured but made no
effort to move from his arms.

"You feel ready," he said throatily as his mouth
made a leisurely journey to hers.

"You should go." But her mouth lifted to meet his.

"Soon." He slid his tongue over her lips and Ellie felt
drugged by sensation. Her bones lost solidity. Her
brain floated in a fog.

"We shouldn't be doing this."

"Why not?" His hands slipped into the front of her
robe and cupped her naked breasts.

A soft moan slipped from her mouth as he caressed
her. "I don't want an emotional involvement, Ben."

He explored her mouth. "All right."

Her robe slid to the floor, and she pressed closer,

seeking more of his tongue and mouth. She was giving in to weakness. She shouldn't let this happen, but she had never wanted anything more. Need for him was growing huge inside her as he moved his hands over her. Her skin tingled wherever he touched her. Dazedly, she thought, so this is what it's like to need a man desperately. She didn't utter a sound of protest when he lifted her into his arms.

Chapter Ten

*M*oonlight silvered the bedroom, softened shadows, wrapped everything in unreality. Ellie lifted her head and found Ben's mouth again. She was floating in a sea of warmth, and it felt so wonderful just to relax and let herself drift. The need for Ben was stirring, expanding, as his strong arms held her naked body crushed against him.

For an instant, as he lowered her to the bed, she thought of trying to fight her way out of the languorous depths.

"Ben—"

Then he kissed her again, and she clung to him, cast adrift in longing. Blindly, her fingers found the buttons of his shirt and undid them as he rained soft kisses on her face and neck. At first the movement of her fingers was tentative, almost shy, but as Ben went on kissing her, his hands caressing her body, she grew more bold. He murmured his pleasure in her ear, husky adoring, encouraging words that soothed her doubts and a-roused her passion.

It seemed to take so long to free him of his shirt. Finally he helped her strip it off, and she ran her hands over the smooth skin of his back. The underlying muscles were hard, strong. She was reassured by his strength. More than anything she wanted him to be strong and sure, because she felt so weak and unsure.

His hands caressed her breasts, and when his mouth joined his hands, Ellie's desire exploded with a quick intake of her breath. Her hands cupped the back of his head to press him closer until his mouth at her breast changed from caressing to greedy. She moved achingly beneath him and her hands, bolder still, worked at his belt buckle.

"Ben, help me . . ." she breathed.

He needed no further encouragement. Briefly he levered himself away from her and stripped off the remainder of his clothing. It required only seconds, but her body glowed with such painful longing that it seemed much longer to Ellie.

With a moan, he lay back down and crushed her against him, flesh against flesh. He ran his hands over her thighs and a rush of heat engulfed her. A heavy sigh of need escaped, and Ben caught it in his mouth as his lips met hers. His gentle, giving hands drove her wild, and she dug her nails into his shoulders. No one had ever made her feel like this—senseless and aching with need to be loved and give herself in return. If she could have formed the words, she would have begged him to take her quickly. But Ben wanted to draw out and add to the pleasure.

His tongue tasted the hollow at the base of her throat before gliding lower to nuzzle her breasts and lower still until she was sure she would lose her mind if he didn't take her.

"Oh, Ben . . . please . . ." The words were a strangled gasp.

Ben had caught glimpses in her before of feminine response, but he was overwhelmed by the unrestrained answer of her body to his lovemaking. Her hungry movements beneath him, the softness of her mouth as she pressed kisses on his shoulders, drove him past the boundaries of his own need. He wanted her to experience everything she was capable of; he wanted her to remember this night always. In the moonlight she looked like every man's most erotic dream, and her skin felt like heated satin under his hands. Her blood throbbed in the pulse that his lips found at the side of her throat, and her need flowed from her into him like the beat of a jungle drum. She moaned his name and reached for him, and the shock of it shot through him with such force that his body vibrated with it. She wanted him. Gratitude and awe mixed with the fire of desire and drove him to the edge of reason.

All thought of drawing out the pleasure any longer fled. His mouth crushed down on hers, and Ellie answered the demand with a desperate hunger that she'd never felt before. There were no restraints now for either of them. Ellie opened herself to the one man who could satisfy the need that raged through her. She gasped against his shoulder as she took him inside her.

The warmth and strength of his body enveloped her as she gave herself up completely and went with him to peaks higher than any she remembered, higher even than she had dreamed of.

Ben spiraled back from the shattering heights. His body felt weighted with lead. For fear of hurting Ellie, he slid off her and, keeping his arms wrapped around her, drew her against his chest. She felt incredibly soft and warm in his arms and too small to comprise a whole world. Yet she was the world to him at that moment. Everything, everybody else seemed so insignificant and far away that they might have faded into nothingness.

The pins that had been half-heartedly confining Ellie's hair had been lost in the bed, and the wavy mass felt like silk beneath Ben's arms, which encircled her back. The moonlight touched her body, making it look like fine marble, but she was warm and malleable in Ben's arms, her breasts cushioned against his chest. He didn't think he would ever want to let her go again. He'd known that beneath her controlled exterior there was passion, but he hadn't guessed its depth or that he would respond to it so completely. He had never felt so close to a woman in his life, or so vulnerable. This woman who had come into his life only weeks ago— who, he'd convinced himself, wasn't his kind of woman —had touched him in places where nobody had penetrated before. He had no defenses against Ellie.

Ellie's head rested on Ben's shoulder, her face turned into the dark hollow of his neck. She felt weightless and lethargic and content. In the nine years of her marriage, she'd never experienced the relinquishment of every restraint, as she just had with Ben. With her husband, even in their moments of intimacy, she'd never lost the sense of trying to be what he wanted her to be; it had been impossible to fully abandon herself to sensation. The realization dawned that she'd never felt like a complete woman before tonight. The warm security of Ben's arms and the clean smell of his skin swaddled her, and she felt protected. She didn't want to let that go for a while yet.

But she didn't want to examine the feeling, either. How well did she know this man who had set her free to be more of a woman than she had ever been before?

"This wasn't supposed to happen," she murmured, and snuggled her face deeper into the curve of his neck.

Her words brought Ben out of a pleasant state of sated drowsiness. He didn't want to say anything to dispel their closeness. After a moment, he said carefully, "It's better when it's not planned."

"Is that why . . ." There was the edge of a smile in her voice, and yet she couldn't bring herself to finish the question. Is that why it was so good?

But Ben heard the unspoken words and held her closer. "I don't think it would have made much difference whether we planned it or not. You're so special, Ellie."

"Am I?" She closed her eyes, feeling so relaxed that she forgot to edit her thoughts before she uttered them.

"Well, if I'd known, I'd have read a book or something."

His hand roamed over the curve of her hip. "What kind of book?" he asked absently.

Sudden shyness intruded into her contentment. She wished she'd been more careful with her words. "You know, one of those manuals that come wrapped in plain brown paper."

His caressing hand stopped as deep laughter rumbled through him. "You're not serious."

"Well . . . yes." Her face had grown hot, and she was thankful for the darkness. She wasn't sure she would ever be able to face Ben again in broad daylight. But she'd bumbled her way into this, and she had to get through it. "I mean, I don't know all the—uh— techniques. I'm sure you've been with much more—uh —adequate women . . ." Her voice trailed off. Every word out of her mouth seemed only to be making matters worse.

"If you were any better, Ellie honey, I'd be in cardiac arrest right now. Where did you get the idea you're inadequate?"

She had always known that Greg had found her lacking in a number of ways. He hadn't said so in so many words, but his constant efforts to improve her spoke more eloquently than a direct accusation. If he had found her exciting in bed, would he have had to look elsewhere? "I don't know. I've just always thought . . ."

He growled angrily, "Enough," and held her away from him so that he could look into her face. The moonlight revealed anxious lines between her brows. Ben's thumb smoothed away the lines, and his other hand brushed the hair away from her face. He caught her chin. "Don't you know what you did to me just now? Couldn't you feel it?"

"I wasn't sure." His sudden anger confused her.

He held her head between his hands and kissed her, and she could feel the anger in him turning to fresh desire. "I wanted you the first time I saw you, even while I was writing you a ticket for running a red light."

"Umm." She kissed the corner of his mouth. His taste thrilled her. "I never would have guessed. You were so stern. I knew you didn't like me, but I didn't know why."

"I thought you were some Texas millionaire's wife up for a little spending spree. Another tourist to add a little more tension to my job. I figured you might as well drop a few bucks into the city's coffers while you were at it."

She traced the outline of his lips with her finger. "You don't like tourists, do you?"

"As long as they behave themselves, I can tolerate them."

"I really didn't see that light, you know."

"I believe you." He kissed her, softly at first and then with more evident hunger. "Oh, Ellie, I can't tell you how many nights I've dreamed of having you in my bed, naked like this."

Curls of heat were tingling over Ellie's skin. "Have you?"

Her mouth opened under the crushing weight of his,

and she responded to his demand with an eagerness that matched his. "Ben . . . you make me feel so desirable. Thank you for that."

"If your husband told you you're inadequate, he's a liar," he muttered. His hands molded all the curves and angles of her body, stroking and searching until she was on fire. "Any man who could hold you like this and not shake with wanting you has something wrong with him. You're a beautiful, desirable woman. Don't ever doubt that again."

He *was* shaking, she could feel the tremors in his limbs. She pulled his head down, her mouth as demanding as his. Her hands wandered everywhere, stroking, needing. She felt him shudder and his arms tightened around her, almost painful in their strength. But she wanted him to crush her, she wanted to meld with him, to be a part of him.

"Ellie, Ellie . . ."

Once more they were lost in each other. He took her back into the swirling mists of passion, led her up and up and, finally, through to the other side.

Ben's weight was heavy on her, and his skin was damp under her palms. They lay replete, wordless for a timeless time.

Finally, Ellie mumbled sleepily, "Ben, you're so . . ." But she couldn't think of a word that was good enough.

He nuzzled her ear and, shifting, gathered her to his side. "Handsome? Debonair?" he provided, his voice husky and teasing in her ear.

She chuckled softly. "That, too." She brought his

arm over her breast and held it there. "I don't know if I can say what I mean. You're just so—so real."

His laugh rumbled in his chest. "Go to sleep, Ellie," he said softly. And within moments they were both sleeping, locked in each other's arms.

Much later, Ellie came half-awake, aware that Ben had moved away from her. She dragged her eyes open, but the moon must have gone behind a cloud, because she could see nothing in the darkness.

She felt for him beside her. "Ben?"

He bent to kiss her and pulled the cover more securely around her. "Shh. Go back to sleep, Ellie. It's almost dawn. I'm going home to change into uniform before I go on duty. I'll lock all the doors behind me."

She was too sleepy to argue. She curled into a ball and slept until the morning sunlight fell upon her face and woke her.

Then she had to rush to get dressed and be downstairs by the time the Vinings arrived. As she fastened buttons, brushed her teeth, and applied makeup, her thoughts were all of Ben. I made love with him, she remembered. In my own bed, I slept with him most of the night. In the clear light of day she was astonished. But, astonished or not, she couldn't really regret what they had shared. Ben had shown her parts of herself that she hadn't known were there. He had been a passionate, gentle lover. Had she the power, would she turn back the clock and erase what had happened? She wasn't at all sure that she would.

But what did Ben think of her this morning? What would she see in his face the next time they met?

Did he have regrets? Is that why he had left while she slept? Oh, it was all so confusing. Thank goodness there was plenty of work to do downstairs. She wouldn't have time to think about Ben.

She shook off a flicker of fear as she made the bed hurriedly and remembered the snake coiled there, as it had been when she'd turned back the sheet the evening before. Before going downstairs, she went through the apartment and checked all the windows, especially the two containing the air conditioning units. The only opening she found was a small tear in the screen on one of the living room windows. She didn't really think a snake could climb up the wall of the mill house and through that tiny hole, but she found some wire and repaired the tear, anyway.

She was just unlocking the front doors to the mill house when the Vinings arrived. "What's this?" Pearl asked, plucking something from behind the brass door pull. She held three perfect yellow roses, their stems wrapped in paper toweling.

Ellie took the roses and held them to her nose. "Umm, aren't they lovely?"

Pearl looked thoughtfully at the private smile that set on Ellie's lips. "Where do you reckon they came from?"

"There doesn't seem to be a card," murmured Ellie, and her heart soared as she remembered that there was a rose bush beside Ben's front door.

They went inside and Ellie put the roses in a slender vase.

"'Pears you got an admirer, Ellie," Jake commented

with a grin as he watched her set the roses on her work counter in the post office. "Has Dennis brought the mail yet this morning?"

Ellie laughed. "No, Jake. Dennis is too young for me, and anyway, he doesn't strike me as the type who would leave flowers without a card."

Pearl snorted, "That's right. Dennis would want to be sure he got the credit. Takes an old-fashioned romantic gentleman to send anonymous gifts, eh, Ellie?"

"If you say so, Pearl." Ben, a romantic? Ellie wouldn't have said so before last night. It seemed she had been as guilty as Ben of judging by appearances.

"Now, when I was a girl," Pearl reminisced, "a young lady's admirers always left baskets of wild flowers outside her door on May Day. Jake left me a basket one time, and that's how I first knew he was sweet on me."

Jake shuffled his feet in embarrassment. "You gonna stand here and gab all day, woman? We got work to do."

Ellie smothered a smile. "You have time for a cup of coffee first, don't you, Jake?"

He grumbled an agreement and Pearl was already reaching for the mugs.

Ellie said, "I had another surprise waiting for me when I got home last night—a nasty one. There was a rattlesnake in my bed."

"Lor' have mercy, Ellie!" Pearl exclaimed.

"I know I locked up before we left yesterday," Jake said defensively.

"Yes, the mill house was locked when I got home," Ellie said. "I was wondering, though . . . did you see anybody go upstairs yesterday while you were here?"

Both the Vinings shook their heads emphatically. "Didn't you have the apartment door locked?"

"Yes," Ellie conceded, "but I suppose someone could pick the lock."

"Nobody went up them stairs while we was here," Pearl said. "I was up front all day, taking care of the post office and customers."

"Well, I don't see how the snake could have gotten upstairs by himself," Ellie said, "especially since he was down under the bedspread and top sheet."

"Never heard of such a thing," Pearl muttered. "What did you do when you found it, Ellie?"

"I called the sheriff. He came over and shot the snake."

Jake sipped his coffee loudly and Pearl frowned at him absently. "There's too many strange things happening around here. Gives me the heebie-jeebies."

"I'm getting a little jumpy myself," Ellie said, smiling in a belated attempt to dispel Pearl's gloom. "The other night during that rainstorm, I actually thought I saw a woman in a white dress on the bridge."

She had meant it as a joke, poking fun at herself. But Pearl's eyes widened in shock and she gasped, "Law, what they say must be true then. Mandy's ghost is haunting the mill!"

Ellie tried to retract. "Oh, no, Pearl. I'm convinced it was an optical illusion. There was thunder and lightning—the rain was pouring down and the wind was blowing tree limbs about. I was nervous about the storm and trying to close the windows . . ." She could see that she wasn't allaying Pearl's unease, and out of desperation, added, "Anyway, why would Mandy's ghost be haunting the mill?"

"Maybe she was murdered," Pearl stated, nodding her head as if the possibility had just occurred to her.

"Nonsense," Jake said. "Nobody was here but the reverend and Mandy, and I know he didn't kill her. He worshipped that girl."

"Well . . ." Pearl pondered for a moment. "Maybe somebody else was murdered here, maybe a long time ago."

"Have you ever heard of other deaths at the mill?" Ellie asked.

"No," Jake put in. "There wasn't any, or we'd have heard about it."

"Jake's right." Pearl sighed. "I've lived near the mill all my life, and I never heard of anybody dying here but Mandy. But I still say, where there's a ghost, there's been something wicked happen."

Jake got to his feet. "I ain't interested in hearing any more about ghosts, Pearl, not unless one of 'em's gonna help me get that work done."

Pearl was not her usual garrulous self for the rest of the day, and Ellie knew she was worried about the mill's being haunted. Too late, she wished she hadn't mentioned seeing the woman on the bridge. Obviously Pearl would not be convinced that the woman had been a trick of the rain and wind.

After closing the mill at five, Ellie put on a jacket and carried a cup of hot tea out to the front steps. She wasn't consciously waiting for Ben to return from work, but when she saw his car rounding the bend in the road, she realized with a jolt that subconsciously she'd been hoping to see him. Ben waved and stopped the car, and immediately, Ellie felt embarrassed. Would he have stopped if she hadn't been sitting there? Did he think she wanted him to stop, that she was waiting for him?

He got out of the car, carrying a paper sack. He saw the confusion and embarrassment in her face as he walked toward her. He found it strangely endearing. He was encouraged by the fact that she was outside and hoped it meant that she'd been waiting for him. Saying nothing, he bent over her and kissed her upturned mouth.

Ellie's hand curved around his arm, taking pleasure from the hardness of his bicep beneath the khaki shirt. He had kissed her so naturally, without a moment's hesitation. He might have felt obligated to stop when he saw her, but he didn't have to kiss her. He had wanted to. Being with him, lifting her lips for his kiss, made her feel a lightness. She wasn't sure what name to give to the feeling. Pleasure? Gratitude? Happiness? Yesterday she wouldn't have thought this easy intimacy possible, but now . . .

He sat beside her and gathered her against him. His face pressed into her hair. "Hi."

"Hi." She shifted, wanting to break the spell before it overwhelmed her. She smiled at him. "Thank you for the roses."

The fragrance of her hair lingered in his nostrils. "How did you know they were from me?"

"Who else could it be? I haven't exchanged more

than a few words with any other man since I came here."

He planted a kiss on the tip of her nose. "I'm gratified to hear that."

She picked up her empty cup from the porch. "I've just had a cup of tea. Would you like one?"

"Not just now." He held out the paper sack. "I brought you something."

Her eyes lifted to his. "Another present? You'll spoil me."

He grinned. "I'd like to spoil you, but wait till you see what it is before you jump to conclusions."

She opened the sack. An evil-looking black handgun lay inside. She thrust the sack into Ben's hand. "I don't want this. I wouldn't know what to do with it."

"I'll teach you," he said solemnly. "I don't want you here alone without some means of protecting yourself." He set the sack beside him on the step.

I should be glad that he finally believes I haven't been imagining the strange happenings at the mill, she thought. His bringing the gun proved it, but it also told her he was concerned that she might come to some harm. It wasn't a very reassuring realization.

"Do you really think it's necessary?"

He nodded. "Better to be safe than sorry. I think you should have all the locks changed, too."

She shivered suddenly, and he gathered her into his arms again. "I'm not trying to frighten you," he went on.

For a few moments, there were only the two of them. There was no intangible menace hanging over the mill as long as she was in Ben's arms. Wordlessly, they held each other.

"I suppose you're right," she murmured, almost wishing he would say that he'd been joking, after all. "I hate the thought, but I'd better learn to use the gun." She shifted her head slightly to see his face. "It's getting colder."

"Mmmm." He nuzzled her throat, losing himself in the softness and fragrance of her. "I could be persuaded to stay for dinner."

She laughed, and he kissed her. She tilted her head back. "Could you? Now what would I have to do to persuade you?"

He grinned. "Whatever turns you on. I'm a pushover."

Still laughing, she got to her feet. "Come on, then."

They joined hands as they climbed the stairs. "What are we having?"

She shook her head at him. "Beggars can't be choosers, Sheriff."

Chapter Eleven

Ben sliced and buttered a loaf of Ellie's homemade French bread and tucked it into the oven while she cooked spaghetti and made the meat sauce. When he passed behind her to get the items needed to set the table, he paused and, lifting her hair, pressed a soft kiss against the sensitive skin of her neck. As she rested her spoon against the side of the pan, she found herself turned and folded into his arms.

His mouth touched hers tenderly in a series of whisper-light kisses. But when she lifted her arms to bring him closer, their lips lingered in a long, hungry kiss. His hands drifted down her sides to rest on her hips. The things those hands had done to her last night played through her mind like a haunting melody. Ben made her feel like a different woman—new, touched by magic. It was too easy to lose her senses in his arms.

Ellie drew back a little to break the spell. "The sauce will burn."

"The sauce isn't the only thing that's burning," he murmured and laughed when she blushed. He stroked the back of his hand across her flushed cheek. "I wondered all day how it would be when we saw each other again."

"So did I."

"It feels right."

She wasn't sure *right* was the word she would have used. *Mad* or *dangerous* would have been more like it. "Yes . . ." She drew away from him and turned to stir the sauce. She heard him opening drawers and taking out placemats and silverware.

He wants to stay the night again, she thought. She left the sauce to simmer and took salad vegetables from the refrigerator. She placed the lettuce and tomatoes on a cutting board and stared at them for a moment. She had been waiting for him when he came from work, and he'd stopped and kissed her, just as though it was what they did every evening. Now they were preparing a meal together. And thinking about making love again.

It was going to happen, and she wasn't going to try to stop it. Why should she when she wanted it so much? With a quick shake of her head, Ellie reached for a knife and began dicing tomatoes.

When the meal was ready, she lit three big, scented candles in the center of the table and turned out the kitchen light. Ben held her chair for her, bending down to kiss her cheek at the corner of her mouth when she was seated. "I like the way your skin looks in candlelight," he murmured. "It's the color of fine pearls."

Ellie smiled at him as he pulled out his own chair. "You're a romantic, Ben."

He sat down, elbows on the table, gazing across at her in the flickering candlelight. "Any man can be a romantic with the proper inspiration."

Ellie laughed and offered him the spaghetti. "That's exactly what I mean. You know how to make a woman feel appreciated."

"You are appreciated, Ellie. More than you can imagine."

She had no idea how to reply to that. She turned the conversation, inquiring about his day. He made a comical tale of being called out to help a farmer look for his straying calves. I feel comfortable with him, Ellie thought. More comfortable than I ever felt in my marriage.

Ben watched the changes in her face as he told her about his day. She was more relaxed than she'd been when he first arrived. He liked making her laugh. He liked preparing meals with her, as though they were married. The word slid into his mind before he even knew it was coming. Married. It was a shock to realize that he could quite easily envision himself married to Ellie. He couldn't remember ever coming to care so deeply for a woman so quickly.

Ben wasn't a man who denied his feelings. Maybe she wasn't the uncomplicated woman his intellect would have chosen, but he was falling in love with Ellie. He wondered how she would feel if she knew? Perhaps he

wasn't being entirely fair to her. She had warned him
that she wanted no emotional entanglements, and he'd
glibly agreed. Her divorce had made her distrustful,
and she would fight her feelings. He would have to be
patient.

They cleaned up the kitchen together and the lovemaking afterward was as deeply moving as it had been
the night before. When Ben led her into the bedroom
and began undressing her, Ellie made no pretense of
having expected anything else. She responded with the
urgency that was pounding in her blood, wrapping her
arms around him, drawing him closer. With impatiently
fumbling hands, Ben stripped off his own clothing. His
mouth locked on hers as they fell onto the bed together.

She was like fluid heat beneath him, and his mouth
was everywhere, tasting, giving, and taking the most
exquisite pleasure. Ellie's body was pliant, greedy to
accept all he had to give. She simply let go and let him
take her wherever he would. Mindless, flowing, she
wrapped herself around him and rushed toward the
mystical oneness they had found the night before.

There was no gentleness in his taking this time, there
was desperation and ravenous hunger, as if they had
been denied each other's bodies for years. She moaned
his name over and over as they rode the wild crest of
their passion together. The blinding response shattered
through them, almost painful in its release, and they lay
limp and drained.

Ben's arms drawing her against him, his hands soothing her damp, heated skin, were gentle now. He kissed
the arch of her brow, the delicate line of her jaw, the

feminine slope of her shoulder. Ellie sighed and snuggled closer to him.

I love you, Ellie. He ached with the need to tell her. He bit his tongue to stop the words from rushing out. It was too soon to tell her. Her old fears would come between them. She might send him away forever. So instead of the words, he gave her tenderness. He made her comfortable in the curve of his body, brushed her brow with gentle kisses, stroked her tangled hair until she fell asleep.

Ellie awoke to the smell of fresh coffee. Ben stood beside the bed, a steaming mug in his hand. "You can't sleep all day, sugar."

She buried her face in the pillow. "It's Sunday."

"And we have work to do."

She turned her head, peering up at him with one eye. "What work?"

"Target practice."

"I should've known you wouldn't forget," Ellie groaned, and sat up, pulling the sheet over her.

"That's my girl," Ben said approvingly and handed her the mug.

The mug warmed her hands and the steaming aroma rising from it tantalized her. She blew on the coffee and sipped cautiously. "Ummm. This is so good."

"Wait there. I'll bring your breakfast."

She lay back against the pillows, smiling. He was so generous, so giving. He was back in a few minutes with a tray. A single plate held a stack of golden pancakes melting with butter and three crisp strips of bacon. He set the tray on her legs.

It was a new experience for Ellie, being waited on so grandly. She stared at the tray. "Ben, you shouldn't have gone to so much trouble. This is terribly sweet." She tilted her face to look up at him, and his mouth was waiting for hers. The kiss was lingering, but light.

"I have my sweet moments."

She laughed. "Your chivalry is exceeded only by your modesty, Sheriff." She bit into a crisp slice of bacon. "Where's your breakfast?"

He settled on the side of the bed as she poured syrup from a small pitcher. "I ate an hour ago."

He had been wandering about her apartment as she slept, making himself at home, making breakfast. She found she rather liked the idea—too much. For the first time, she noticed that he was wearing jeans and a plaid shirt. "Did you go home for a change of clothing?"

"No, these were in the car."

She stifled a desire to ask if he always carried a change of clothing in his car, or if he'd made plans to spend the night with her the previous morning when he left for work. She didn't want to know if he'd planned it. She knew it was unreasonable, but she felt less committed, believing that last night had merely "happened." It was less unnerving to think that they had been carried away by feelings too strong to be denied; it relieved her of responsibility.

Face it, Ellie, you're having an affair. One night, you might have been able to dismiss as a loss of judgment in a rush of loneliness and overwhelming passion. But two nights? That's a little hard to swallow.

Ben considered her lowered eyes. Her concentrated

attention to her breakfast seemed to shut him out. "I always carry extra clothes in the car, Ellie. There are times when I have to work all night without a chance to go back home."

"Does that happen often?"

"No."

He had realized what she was thinking, and she realized he was hurt by it. She slipped a forkful of pancake dripping with syrup into her mouth and chewed fastidiously. "I'll be ready in ten minutes. I'm a fast dresser."

He laughed and shook his head. "That works out fine, then. I'm a fast undresser."

Ellie lifted an eyebrow. "You haven't any shame at all, Sheriff."

"Not much," he agreed.

She finished her breakfast and handed him the tray. "Thank you for a delightful breakfast. Did you make those pancakes from scratch?"

"Nope, I got a sack of griddle-cake mix from downstairs. Not that I couldn't have made them from scratch, if the mix hadn't been so handy."

She tilted her head, assessing him. "I've never known a man like you before."

He lifted a hand to her hair and rumpled it more severely than it had been upon awaking. "Nor I a woman like you, Ellie." The thought seemed to please him. He was smiling as he left the bedroom with the tray.

Ben set up a cardboard target behind the mill house and instructed Ellie in loading, aiming, and firing the pistol. She used up two dozen shells before she was able to hit the cardboard and Ben decided she could quit.

"This has been a waste of time, really," Ellie told him. "I don't think I could ever shoot another human being."

"With any luck, you'll never have to. Just the threat of using it will scare off an intruder." He was reloading the pistol. Finished, he engaged the safety catch. "I'm going to put this in the drawer of your bedside table. Then we can go for a walk. Game?"

"Sure. I'll wait here for you."

They walked for almost two hours, admiring the blaze of autumn leaves in the woods and stopping frequently to watch a squirrel or a rabbit or to listen to a birdcall.

Ben took her to the cliff over which the hunter had fallen the previous year so she'd know where it was and be cautious when walking nearby.

"Let's go back the other way now," he said, taking her hand. "I'll show you the Gunter cabin."

"Pearl says Priscilla Gunter wanders off at night." Unaccountably the memories of a woman singing in the dark woods returned with such clarity that Ellie almost thought she was hearing it again.

He tucked her hand with his into the pocket of his Windbreaker. "She'd be better off in a nursing home, but she's harmless."

Ellie nodded, thinking about the woman in white she'd seen on the bridge. Had it been an optical illusion? Or had Priscilla gotten lost in the storm? "Oliver has befriended Jimmy Gunter. He's trying to persuade Jimmy to tell you what happened to the things stolen from the high school. He thinks Jimmy would have told already, but he's afraid of the Crowder brothers." .

Ben lifted a shoulder. "I'm surprised. After our last meeting, I didn't think Hilderbrand would do anything to help the department."

"He told me that you were pretty tough on him."

"It's my job, Ellie."

She flashed him a thoughtful look. "That wasn't meant as a criticism, just a statement of fact. But Oliver doesn't strike me as the type to hold grudges. Besides, I think he's more concerned with helping Jimmy than the sheriff's department. He needs to feel needed, Ben." She stepped over a fallen branch in the path. "I've been wondering . . . Oliver seems to enjoy working with young people. Isn't there some youth program in Springville where he could help as a volunteer?"

Ben's eyes held a mixture of amusement and approval. "I wonder if Hilderbrand realizes what a good friend he has in you."

"You won't tell him I asked, will you? If there is such a program, you could just mention it to him casually the next time you see him."

He squeezed her hand. "There's a youth hotline. I'll get the particulars and let him know about it. If he's interested, he can take it from there."

She tilted her face to his. "Thank you, Ben."

He halted and, placing his hands on her shoulders, turned her to him. He studied her face, his eyes searching. "You continue to surprise me. I'd think, with everything that's been happening to you, you'd have enough to worry about without taking on Oliver Hilderbrand."

"It's easier to find solutions to somebody else's problems. Sometimes I just hope that if I ignore what's been happening to me, it'll go away."

His eyes were deeply intense. "You're really troubled about what's been happening at the mill, aren't you?"

"Yes," she agreed, then slipped her arms around him to hold him tightly. The gesture disarmed him. Ellie closed her eyes and pressed her cheek against his shoulder. "I try not to let it bother me too much, but I don't always succeed. During that last rainstorm we had, I thought I saw a woman in a white dress crossing the bridge behind the mill house."

"Ellie, I didn't realize . . ." he murmured into her hair. A tremor passed through her, and he tightened his arms around her.

"I made the mistake of telling Pearl," she went on in a small voice, "and now she's convinced that Mandy's ghost is haunting the mill. I tried to tell her I probably hadn't seen anything. It was only a trick of light."

"Do you honestly believe that?"

She lifted her face. "Yes, I have to." As his mouth touched hers she thought fleetingly that she could feel safe in the mill house if Ben were there every night. It was a dangerous thought, and the sensible part of her told her not to come to depend on Ben. Keep it light, keep it casual.

When they started walking again, he said, "What you need is to get away from here, completely forget about the mill. Let's go to Silver Dollar City next Sunday."

Still troubled by her earlier thoughts, Ellie told herself that things were moving far too fast. "Could I let you know later in the week?"

There was a retreat in her tone. A barrier had gone up. She didn't want to be pushed too hard. Ben recognized this and said carelessly, "Sure."

They came upon the Gunter cabin, sitting in a small clearing. There was no sign of life, except for the smoke curling from the chimney, and they passed by without stopping. Although Ellie's hand was laced through his, Ben sensed that the distance she had put between them when he'd mentioned plans for next Sunday was still there. He wanted to shake her and take her to bed and reclaim the closeness that had been between them last night. He knew that he could make her want him, but he also knew that afterward, when he'd gone home, she might resent him. Ellie hadn't come to grips with her feelings about him yet, whatever they were. The best thing he could do for her right now was to give her space.

When they got back to the mill house, he said, "I won't come inside with you, Ellie. I know you'd like to be alone." He could see the quick flicker of gratitude as she digested his words. "I'll call you later."

"Thank you," she murmured, and gave in to the urge to touch his mouth with hers one more time before he left.

The mill house seemed extraordinarily big and empty and echoing when he was gone. Singing to herself for company, Ellie hung the ruffled curtains she'd bought in Rogers the last time she'd made deliveries. Still unwilling to pay the price of having draperies made from Liz's handmade fabric, she had bought enough inexpensive, sill-length cotton priscillas for the whole apartment—beige for the living room and bedroom, brown for the bath, and bright tangerine for the kitchen. It took most of the afternoon, but the apartment had acquired a distinct personality by the time she had finished. The saucy curtains, added to the baskets and pots of green plants and autumn leaves, turned it into a real home—Ellie's home.

Pleased with herself, she decided to check the downstairs for cracks and holes where mice might come in. Even though Jake had assured her he'd filled all the cracks, she didn't have complete faith in his eyesight and wouldn't be satisfied until she'd checked herself. She went downstairs with a box of steel wool and made a slow, methodical inspection. She found only two tiny cracks between the wall and floor behind the grain bins and she pushed steel wool into them with a knife. They were probably too small to admit a mouse, but she felt better after they were filled. To further ease her mind, Jake had scattered the rat poison outside. The mill should now be safe from all varieties of rodents.

She went back upstairs, thinking about the scrapings of mortar she'd found outside next to the foundation. Another thing that had never been explained to her satisfaction.

She was hardly aware that dusk had settled while she worked until she entered the darkened apartment. She stood in the living room, from which the light had faded, and the silence swirled around her like water. She felt a prickling at the base of her skull.

She was tired from hanging the curtains and crawling

about downstairs in search of cracks. She told herself that that was why she felt suddenly as though she were being watched. She was overtired.

Shaking off the feeling, she flipped on some lights and went through the apartment to admire the curtains again. The scrapings of mortar had been made by an animal. She had been convinced of that earlier, so why was she now doubting that explanation? What if the scraping had been done by someone trying to get inside the foundation? But that didn't make sense. Why would anyone want to do that? She sighed. Perhaps it would be easier if she, like Pearl, could assign all unexplainable phenomena to ghosts.

She had always had feelings about houses—each one gave off its own special aura, some much more forcefully than others. But she could not take that final step into believing that certain places were haunted.

Still, was it possible that houses held the residue of past events that had occurred within their walls? Feelings. Impressions. Did vibrations of violence linger where murder had been done? Could that explain the vague sense she sometimes had of another presence in the mill house?

But there had been no unnatural death at the mill except for Mandy's. Unless . . .

Nobody had ever told her exactly where Mandy's father had died. Was it near here? And what of the baby William Swafford, whose body had never been found? Had somebody buried the body close by? But if it was buried, that could mean that whoever did it had killed the child and wanted the evidence hidden. Had William Swafford been murdered at the mill?

Ellie heard her heart thudding in her ears. Wrenching her mind away from the ill-fated Swafford family, she strode purposefully back to the living room and turned on the television news.

Ben didn't call until Wednesday. It had only been three days, but she had missed him more than she would have thought possible. When he asked to take her out to dinner Wednesday night, she accepted without a moment's hesitation. During dinner, they made plans for the trip to Silver Dollar City Sunday. Ellie couldn't remember why she had been hesitant earlier about going.

It was late when they returned to the mill house. They shared a bottle of wine and made love, and Ellie fell into a dreamless sleep in Ben's arms. Hours later, when he left her bed before dawn, she had to bite her tongue to keep from asking him to stay.

Ben had to go to Little Rock at the end of the week, but he called her every day and Ellie found herself looking forward to their phone conversations with the breathless anticipation of an adolescent. She almost forgot what it was like to be alone. When she let herself think about it, it worried her that she was coming to rely on Ben's companionship. But she shoved the worry aside and looked forward to Sunday.

She could make it on her own, she told herself. She no longer ached with humiliation when she thought about Greg. She had depended on Greg and he had let her down, but she'd survived. She could see now that she had defined herself through her husband, and when that identity was torn away she'd had to carve out another for herself alone. She would never reject her own personality and needs to please someone else again. But what was wrong with enjoying Ben's company as long as he wanted to be with her?

It seemed much longer than a week since she and Ben had first made love. At times, she felt as though she had known him, needed him, always. She was still wary, still keeping a rein on her emotions. But Ben was filling more and more of her thoughts.

On Sunday they left early in the morning for Branson, arriving at Silver Dollar City before ten.

Whether it was being with Ben or getting away from the mill for the day, or a combination of the two, Ellie didn't know. But she couldn't remember when she had enjoyed herself so much or laughed so often.

She was enchanted by the woodcarvers' building and spent over an hour browsing through the two floors.

They had lunch at a restaurant on the grounds, and after they were seated at a small table, Ben brought out a wood carving of a funny old Ozark moonshiner.

"For me?" Ellie squealed with delight.

"I don't see anybody else around here, do you?"

She gave him an arch look. "He'll be the first in my collection of Ozark wood carvings. Thank you." She studied the moonshiner happily before slipping him into her purse.

When the waitress had taken their order, she went on, "I haven't heard from Liz in a while. We used to talk on the phone a couple of times a week, but I haven't been able to catch her at home lately."

"Hank Rushmore is monopolizing her time." Ben shook his head as if he found this hard to believe. "Darned if I don't think Liz is falling for old Tubby."

"I've gotten the same impression. Will he hurt her?"

Ben laughed. "From what I've seen, Hank is still mad about her. Supposedly he came home for the reunion, but that was more than a week ago. He's got a business to run, but he's still in Springville. It wouldn't surprise me to hear they're making wedding plans."

"I hope Liz doesn't rush into something she may come to regret."

"Have you lost your faith in marriage?"

She shifted her gaze away from his intent regard. "I just don't think people should go into it with false expectations."

"Is that what you did?"

She made herself look at him steadily. "I expected to live happily ever after. Greg expected to wave a magic wand and turn me from an ordinary girl into a princess. It didn't work out that way. He found himself another princess."

She looked so unhappy. He wanted to hold her and tell her how precious she was to him. "Doesn't Greg realize he's totally crazy?"

His indignation made Ellie smile. "No," she said lightly, and drew a deep breath. "Could we talk about something else?"

"Yes, I think we'd better. How are things at the mill?"

Ellie didn't want to tell him that she hadn't slept well the past two nights. She had lain awake, trying to identify every noise, as every frightening thought she'd

ever had about the mill flitted through her mind. She
had needed to get away. Ben had seen that days before
she had.

"Business is okay, but I needed to get away from it. I
needed to be with you," she admitted.

His hand covered hers on the table. "So did I." He
lifted her hand and kissed her palm. He raised his head,
folding her fingers over the place he'd kissed. "You're
the first thing I think of when I wake up in the morning,
Ellie."

His solemn look made Ellie feel giddy. She smiled.
"May I tell you something, Sheriff?"

"Anything."

Ellie gazed at their clasped hands. "I feel like me
when I'm with you."

"That's the nicest thing you've ever said to me,
love."

He said the last word like a caress, and Ellie's heart
turned over. He had never called her that before. She
looked into his eyes and saw fathomless depths of
emotion. It was there clearly for her to read. He was
thinking about making love to her. And suddenly she
was thinking about it, too.

Chapter Twelve

It was almost midnight when they arrived back at the mill.

"I still can't get over some of those wood carvings," Ellie said as Ben fitted the key in the front door lock. "I've never considered myself artistic, but I'm thinking of buying some tools and learning to carve."

"I got the fever once and tried to carve a duck decoy," Ben said. "It looked more like a blue jay than a duck. But my tools are still around somewhere. You can borrow them."

"You gave up after one carving?" she inquired as they started up the stairs.

"I didn't have the patience for it." In the apartment, Ben slipped out of his jacket and tossed it into a chair.

She gave him a speculative look. "You probably didn't want it enough. Would you like a brandy?"

"Yes." He followed her into the kitchen and watched her fix the drinks. "If you're serious about carving, there's a man in Springville who gives lessons."

"Really?" She turned back with two wine glasses. "I remembered to get the brandy, but forgot snifters."

"It'll taste just as good." Taking the brandy from her, Ben led her to the living room couch.

Greg, she thought, would have taken the opportunity to correct her hostessing *faux paus* if she'd ever served brandy in wine glasses in their home. Poor Greg, he was always so concerned with correctness. Ah, well, she sighed to herself, let him drive Cynthia crazy now. She settled into the curve of Ben's arm. "What's his name?"

His hand toyed idly with a strand of her hair. "Who?"

"The man who teaches wood carving," she murmured, drowsy now with contentment.

"Abner Dwyer. He's in his eighties but he still takes a few promising students. He's got a shop in his home." His fingers curved lightly along the side of her neck.

"Maybe I'll just get an instruction book first. Then if I seem to have a knack, I'll go and see him." Ellie let her head fall back against his shoulder. She never felt so content as when Ben's arm was around her. "After the tourist season, when I have more time. My customers are already starting to dwindle slowly. Jake says by the middle of November we'll be lucky to have five customers a day outside of locals. The Vinings are going to work only two or three days a week this winter . . ."

He listened to the soft murmur of her voice, already dreading the moment when he would have to leave her. How quickly she had come to mean so much to him. He would never have believed it possible that first day when she drove into town in her Mercedes. It was no longer enough to hold her, to make love to her. He wanted to share the daily routine of her life, to make plans for them together. He wanted, needed more than an affair with Ellie. There were moments, such as now, when he came so close to blurting out his true feelings and asking her to marry him. He didn't know how much longer he could be cautious and bide his time.

He set down his drink, and then hers. Ellie gazed mistily up at him as she lifted her face for his kiss. As if sensing her need for tenderness, his mouth savored hers with such sweet gentleness that it brought tears to her eyes. He pressed her back against the cushions of the couch and the lovemaking continued at an unhurried, dreamy pace.

Her hands felt the texture of his hair, then followed the corded muscles at the back of his neck to the broad, hard shoulders. Murmuring her sleepy pleasure, she continued to explore his body through his clothing—his arms, his back, his lean hips.

With exquisite slowness, Ben unbuttoned her blouse and spread it open to find her breast. His languorous kisses kept her drugged and drifting somewhere in space as his fingers stroked the curve of her breast to the peak. Gently he manipulated the nipple and it hardened between his fingers.

"You're so beautiful." His voice was thick with desire.

His lips enclosed the thrusting peak, and Ellie's dreamy pleasure was quickly infused with urgency. She moved beneath him and cradled his head in her hands and kissed his hair. "Ben . . . oh, Ben, I need you so much . . ."

The husky words seemed to snap the thread of Ben's control. He groaned and his mouth found hers fiercely and he pressed her into the cushions with the hard length of his body. Their mouths remained locked on each other as he stripped off her clothing. Wanting to feel more of his flesh, Ellie whimpered and tugged at his sweater. With an impatient sound, he left her briefly to pull off his sweater and jeans.

Then he was on top of her again, his body heating her, and his mouth was everywhere, and Ellie's hands roamed restlessly over his body, touching, needing. She kissed his jaw, his neck, his shoulder, loving the taste of his skin in her mouth. They were shaken by passion broken free from all restraints.

He took her on the couch, and Ellie moaned with a desperation that went on and on. She was shuddering as the release started, and she heard his labored breath in her ear. She wrapped herself around him, needing his solid strength as well as the masculine weakness that came as he lost himself and cried out her name.

They lay together, limp and pliant. His passion satisfied for the time, Ben's love welled up inside him, demanding utterance. Aching with the tenderness she brought out in him, he let his hand glide over her damp skin, felt the delicate bones beneath the smooth flesh. He kissed her damp brow.

Ellie sighed, moving as close to him as she could get. He stroked her hair, pressing her head against his shoulder.

"I love you." He hadn't meant to say it yet. But whatever caution he might have exercised had been lost in the afterglow of their lovemaking. She grew very still in his arms. Her silence troubled him, and he said, "Look at me, Ellie."

Slowly, she lifted her head, and he held her eyes with his. "I love you." He wished that he could speak eloquently of his love, could make her understand how deeply he meant it.

But more eloquent words were not needed. Ellie saw it all in his eyes, and inside her joy and fear warred with each other, pulling at her from opposite directions. She shook her head. "Don't," she whispered. "Please . . . you can't."

He didn't know what he had expected, but not the near-panic he heard in her voice. "I can't stop myself." The fear in her eyes twisted a painful knot inside him. "It's far too late for that." How could he sound so calm when he felt so hurt and frustrated?

"Let me go." She pushed him away and sat up, reaching for her blouse. Her hands shook as she buttoned it. Nine years of anxiety rushed at her from all sides. Recent resolutions raised their heads to remind her of her failure to keep them. "I don't want you to love me."

Love. It ended in such pain and self-doubt. If only he hadn't said the word. . . . She'd been fooling herself—

there was no way to have the joy without risking the disaster. She couldn't go through that again.

"What you want doesn't have much to do with it, it seems." He would have reached out to touch her, but she looked so withdrawn sitting there, her eyes averted, her body half turned from him. If he touched her now, it would be to shake her.

Hurting and angry, Ben dressed, his back to her. She was still sitting on the couch when he turned around, but she'd put on the rest of her clothes while he dressed. She looked up at him with sorrowful eyes. Unable to stop himself, he gripped her shoulders and pulled her to her feet. "Dammit, Ellie! I love you, and I'm not going to stop simply because you tell me to. What do you think has been going on the past few weeks? How did you think this would end? Surely you've guessed that I was falling in love with you."

"Ben, please . . ." His accusing eyes made her feel cold and bereft. More than anything, she wanted him to take her into his arms and tell her everything would be all right. "I didn't let myself think about it." Her clenched stomach throbbed with pain, and it felt as if something had lodged in her throat. Her heart pounded too loudly. She couldn't think clearly. If only she'd had some warning, time to prepare for this. She struggled against the demand his declaration of love put on her. It frightened her, but the thought of losing him tore at her heart. "I don't see why we can't go on as we have been—for now," she whispered miserably.

"How long?" She could hear the anger and accusation in his voice, and she hardened herself against it. She was her own woman. She was making her own choices, doing something with her life that she wanted to do. Love was an added element that she wasn't ready to handle yet, and she wouldn't let Ben push her into something before she was ready.

"I don't see how you can expect me to answer that."

"This isn't a casual affair with me, Ellie," he said deliberately. "I'm not willing to be kept hanging indefinitely. I want a future with you. I know you went through a bad time with your husband, and I'm trying to make allowances for that. I just don't know how long I can keep doing it."

"I'm sorry." Tears were very close and she swallowed desperately. "I can't make promises I might not be able to keep. I can't give you something I don't have. I tried it with Greg, but never again." She knew that if she kept looking at him, she was going to fling herself into his arms. So she turned away, her back rigid, her hands clenched together and trembling.

He neither moved nor spoke for a long moment. He hadn't hurt like this since—well, he couldn't remember when. With deliberate movements, he reached for his jacket and put it on. He had to get out of there before he said or did something he'd be sorry for. He had known it was too soon to speak. Now all he could do was get out and leave her alone, as she wanted. He paused at the door. *I love you, Ellie, but I'll learn to live without you if I have to.* He didn't say good-bye as he shut the door behind him.

The finality of the door's closing turned Ellie around. She stared at the wood panel, hearing his steps on the stairs going farther away. Finally there was the muffled thud of the downstairs door closing. The soft sound of her weeping was swallowed up by the huge silence.

It was the longest night Ellie had ever lived through. She didn't sleep for what seemed an eternity, and when she finally did, it was in fitful catnaps for the remainder of the night.

She shouldn't have let Ben go like that. She should've talked to him, tried to make him understand. But he had wanted to hear that she loved him, too. Failing that, what could she have said that would have made any difference? Things had moved too fast for her. Another man might have been content to drift along in their present relationship indefinitely. Not Ben. As she had come to know him better, she'd realized that he wasn't a man who engaged in casual affairs. He had a lot to give a woman, and he expected a lot in return. With Ben, it would have to be all or nothing, and maybe that's what scared her so much. She wanted to be with him, she needed him. But she wasn't yet ready to risk calling it love, with all that that word meant to Ben. Perhaps she never would be. And perhaps she wouldn't have the chance. Would Ben cut her out of his life now?

She cried again before falling asleep. She awoke later to stare into the darkness, wondering if she'd been awakened by a sound or the troubled anxiety of her dreams. There—she thought she heard a noise from below. A faint, shuffling sound, as if something crept stealthily across the floor downstairs.

She sat up and quietly slid open the drawer of the

bedside table. Her fingers closed over the cold metal of the gun Ben had given her. She waited, hardly daring to breath, listening to the crowding silence. But the sound didn't come again.

She turned on the lamp, put on her robe, and carrying the gun, went through the apartment, turning on more lights. But she knew she wouldn't be able to sleep again until she'd checked downstairs. Gathering all her courage, she unlocked the apartment door, turned on the downstairs lights, and went down the stairs.

There was no sign of anyone having been there. Nothing was disturbed. The doors were still locked. She had put off calling a locksmith to change the locks, telling herself that the only thing inside the locked mill house with her was her own apprehension. Now she realized that new locks would at least give her peace of mind. She'd call a locksmith tomorrow.

She went back to bed, fell asleep again to dream of snakes that hissed her name from the grass as she passed. She tried to run, but her feet were too heavy to do more than stumble along. When she finally reached the mill house, exhausted, she found that the snakes had arrived there before her and slithered across the floor and over the grain bins. She woke herself with a terrified cry that echoed in her ears long minutes after she'd left the dream behind.

She ran her hands over her face and through her hair. She was perspiring. She threw back the covers and reached out to turn the luminous dial of the clock so that she could read it. Five-thirty. She felt as weary as if she hadn't been to bed at all. But sleep might mean more nightmares. She got up and dressed for the day.

Downstairs, she made coffee and straightened drawers and dusted in the post office while she waited for dawn. It came slowly, the slate at the windows giving way to dove-gray, then fading into white, and finally, a lackluster blue. The simple, manual tasks freed her mind to think about her situation with more objectivity than she had been able to muster during the night.

She would find the right time to talk to Ben and try to make him understand her reluctance to move closer to a commitment now. It wasn't fair of him to expect more with what she was going through at the mill. Somehow she had to clear up that situation. Determinedly, she put her mind to sorting through all the frightening, unexplained happenings again and, for the dozenth time, tried to find a common rational thread running through them all.

She considered as dispassionately as possible the thought of death, but discarded it almost immediately. If she had been marked for murder, it would already have been done. She was alone in the mill house more hours of every twenty-four than not. There had been ample opportunity for killing.

Someone was merely trying to frighten her out of the mill; that seemed fairly obvious. But why? She'd already discarded Ben's idea that Oliver Hilderbrand regretted his agreement with her and wanted the mill back. Surely Oliver knew her well enough by now to understand that he wouldn't have to go to such lengths. But just in case he didn't, she would tell him plainly the next time she saw him that she would let him out of the agreement without penalty if he'd changed his mind. She didn't want the mill at the cost of Oliver's unhappiness.

What of Ben's suspicion that it had been Jimmy Gunter who had gotten in and turned on the mill wheel? Could Jimmy be behind everything that had happened? He'd have to have a key—but Oliver had said Jimmy had worked with him in restoring the mill. Perhaps Jimmy had gotten his hands on a key and had a copy made without Oliver's knowledge. Could he have persuaded a girlfriend to masquerade as Mandy's ghost? Possible. Remote, but possible.

Now, why would Jimmy want her out of the mill?

Something around the mill that he didn't want anyone to find, something he'd left there while working for Oliver? That idea seemed too full of holes to be feasible. She had left the mill unattended for several nights while delivering orders, and just yesterday she'd been with Ben in Branson all day until midnight. Whoever was trying to scare her must be watching the mill. He'd know when she was gone. But perhaps he hadn't wanted to risk coming in the daytime, for fear of being seen. So why hadn't he come at night?

Could it be something that couldn't be gotten to easily? Something that would require a good deal of uninterrupted time and labor to reach? Something buried . . .

In the attic? Under the floorboards? Behind a wall?

A thought was trying to edge its way into Ellie's consciousness. Something she'd heard someone say . . .

She put on a jacket and went outside to shake out the dust cloth with which she'd cleaned the post office counter and mail boxes. The morning was clear and crisp. The surrounding foliage was at the height of its beauty, radiant with color. Reluctant to go back inside immediately, she tucked the dust cloth into her jacket pocket and walked around the mill house, trying to make her mind a blank so that the elusive memory would come.

Traces of the poison powder Jake had sprinkled around the foundation could still be seen. On the north side of the mill, Ellie halted. Mortar scrapings littered the dark earth much more thickly than she remembered. Somebody had been at the foundation again, and quite recently.

She recalled Oliver telling her about the restoration work he'd done on the mill. *That whole north wall had slipped off the foundation. Had to rebuild it completely.* And Jimmy had helped him.

Suppose Jimmy had hidden something between the foundation walls and, somehow—perhaps he hadn't come to work for a few days—Oliver had rebuilt that section of the wall before Jimmy could retrieve it, effectively sealing off the hiding place. Or maybe Jimmy hadn't wanted to retrieve it.

As a scenario, it sounded fairly reasonable, but what on earth could Jimmy have wanted to divest himself of a few months ago that he was now trying to reclaim, and in such secrecy? Something that he now wanted to get his hands on so desperately that he was willing to risk being caught trespassing and scheming to force the mill's present occupant out.

She heard the Vinings truck rattling toward her and, as she turned to go back to the front door, something seemed to click into place in her mind. There could be only one answer to what Jimmy Gunter was after.

"Have a nice weekend, Ellie?" Pearl called as she climbed down from the truck.

Except for the ending, but now wasn't the time to think about that. "Yes. You?"

"Tolerable," Pearl replied.

Jake was tucking something into his overalls pocket before getting out of the truck. Tobacco. After a moment, he followed Pearl to the front steps.

"Jake," Ellie said, "would you come around to the back of the mill before you go in? There's something I want to show you."

"I'll get things started," Pearl offered, and went inside.

"See that?" Ellie asked when they had reached the north side of the mill. "Somebody's been digging at the mortar again recently, probably yesterday while I was away. I think he came back last night, but I heard him before he could get to work and turned on the lights. Must have scared him off."

Jake squatted on his haunches and squinted his eyes in order to see better. "Sure looks like something's been at it again." He peered up at her. "You give up the notion it's a rat?"

Ellie cocked her head. "Did you ever really believe that, Jake?"

He grinned sheepishly. "Well, it's kinda farfetched, I admit."

"Right." She paused to consider briefly whether to tell him what she believed or try to concoct another reason for asking him to dig into the foundation. But she couldn't think of anything that wouldn't sound even more bizarre than the truth. "It's a person, and I think I know who."

He straightened up and, pulling out his tobacco plug, bit a piece off the end. "You gonna keep me in suspense?"

She looked at the foundation. "I think it's Jimmy Gunter."

Jake chewed meditatively. "What makes you think so?"

She lifted her shoulders slightly. "He helped Oliver work on rebuilding the mill. Oliver told me himself that this north wall was off the foundation when he started work. It would've been easy for Jimmy to hide something in the foundation that he was afraid to keep at home."

"Wait a minute . . ." Jake drew out the words, pondering what she'd said. "The goods them boys stole from the high school ain't never been found."

Ellie nodded. "That's what I've been thinking. The other boys might have given Jimmy possession of the goods until they thought it was safe to sell it. But Jimmy must have been afraid to keep it at home, for fear his grandmother would find it. So, he could have left it here, probably intending to get it before that section of the wall was rebuilt. I don't know how it happened, but evidently he didn't get it out in time or maybe he didn't want to before. Now, for some reason, he wants it back."

Jake's cloudy eyes regarded her with admiration. "Could be, Ellie."

"Oliver told me he's been trying to talk Jimmy into turning over the goods to the sheriff. Maybe Jimmy has decided to do it."

Jake cogitated, chewing. "If he wanted to do that, why wouldn't he just tell Ben where it is and let the law get it out?"

Ellie had thought of that, too, and she had no good answer. "I don't know. Maybe that's not it. Maybe he's decided to sell it." She shoved her hands into the pockets of her slacks. "Jake, how hard would it be to remove several of these foundation stones? Enough to be able to see if there's anything inside."

Jake spit a stream of tobacco juice and cackled. "I seen that comin', Ellie. Well, I have to admit I'm as curious as you are to see if you're right. We got a chisel and hammer in the mill. I reckon I could get it done in a few hours."

"Good," Ellie breathed. "I'll help Pearl and you can work out here all day."

Jake went inside for the tools, and Ellie explained to Pearl what he was going to do.

Pearl was emptying a basket of wheat into the proper bin. "Wouldn't put it past that Jimmy," Pearl commented, "to have the loot hid here all this time. The boy's grown up without any supervision. It's a cryin' shame, that's what it is."

"I'll help you with that in a minute," Ellie said. "First I'm going to call a locksmith and have all the locks changed."

Pearl sent her a slow, studious look. "Wouldn't hurt. Somebody put that rattlesnake in your bed. I've always said that."

Ellie was glad that Pearl didn't seem to be in one of her ghost-story moods. After she talked to the locksmith, and he agreed to come out to the mill that afternoon, she took Jake's place beside Pearl at the millstone. When the mill work was caught up just before noon, she went outside to help Jake, leaving Pearl to wait on customers.

By mid-afternoon, they had loosened stones in a rough three-feet-square section of the foundation. With the help of the chisel and an iron bar, they wedged the stones out, one by one, piling them to one side.

"It's gonna take another day to put these all back," Jake said as they dropped the last stone into the pile.

"Do you mind?" Ellie asked.

He was squinting into the hole they'd made in the foundation. "Naw, I'd just as soon be doing that as grinding meal. Looks like this has been filled with a lot of little stones."

The two of them began digging out the fill rock with their hands. They had been working for about a quarter hour when Ellie's fingers touched something that didn't feel like rock.

"I think I've found something, Jake."

Carefully, they removed the stones surrounding the object. Jake shook his head, muttering, "Uh—uh—"

Ellie blinked and looked and blinked again. It wasn't a camera or tape recorder. It was bones. The skeleton of a small child.

"Good Gawd!" Jake exclaimed, finally taking in what they had uncovered. "It's a baby! No tellin' how long it's been in here. How in tarnation . . . ?"

He looked at Ellie and she put her hand on his arm, as if to steady herself. His muslin shirt was wet with sweat and stuck to his arm. She drew a breath and expelled it slowly. Jake thrust his hand out, bracing himself against the wall. Evidently they arrived at the same conclusion simultaneously, for he didn't seem surprised when she said, "Jake, I think we've found William Swafford's body."

Chapter Thirteen

"Don't touch it," Jake warned. "We better call the sheriff before we do anything."

"Yes, you're right." Ellie went back inside to tell Pearl what they'd found and phone Ben's office.

He hesitated for a moment when he heard her voice. "I didn't expect to hear from you."

Ellie closed her eyes, wishing she could tell him how much she cared, wishing she knew how to make him understand. She could see him sitting forward in his chair, his expression ranging from surprise to anxiety. She couldn't picture his surroundings. Foolishly, she felt cheated because she had never seen his office. "There's a problem out here at the mill."

"What kind of problem?" he asked almost warily.

And then, as if a frightening thought had just occurred to him, he said, "Are you all right?"

"I'm fine," she assured him. "It's just—Jake and I dug into the mill foundation—"

"You what?"

"It's too involved to explain on the telephone, Ben. I called to tell you we found a body in the foundation—a skeleton."

"A skeleton," he said blankly.

"A human skeleton."

"Oh." He paused as if to reorient himself. "I'll be there as soon as I can. Don't try to move it."

She hung up and went back outside. Pearl hovered over the gaping hole, craning to look down into the foundation, her lips pursed, her hands on her hips. Jake had squatted on one of the huge loose stones, his arms resting on his knees, his gnarled hands clasped.

"Ben said we shouldn't try to move it," Ellie cautioned.

Pearl straightened. Her face was pale. A spot of red set on each cheek. "The thought never entered my mind."

"Little William," Jake mused. "Poor little fella. Reckon how long he was down in there before he died?"

"Don't like to think about it," Pearl stated.

Nor did Ellie. The Vinings were assuming that the child had fallen into the exposed foundation and been unable to get out, that he had starved to death, which would be grisly enough. But any minute one of them would think of the possibility that somebody had put William there and left him, and that was even worse.

Pearl turned away from the hole and leaned back against the mill, arms folded in front of her. "This explains a lot."

Jake squinted up at her curiously. "Well, enlighten us, woman, if you know so much. It don't explain a thing to me ceptin' William wasn't et up by coyotes, like we always thought."

Healthy color was slowly returning to Pearl's face. "I mean Mandy's ghost."

"What about it?" Ellie asked, only half attending, her mind still on how William could have gotten between the foundation walls.

"This explains why she's haunting the mill," Pearl went on, as though she were explaining something quite mundane, like quilting. "She wants William's body found and given a decent burial. Now she'll be able to rest in peace. I don't expect you'll be bothered by any more eerie happenings around here, Ellie."

Ellie wasn't the slightest bit consoled.

Ben arrived a half hour later, followed by a young man in a khaki law officer's uniform and a paunchy older man in a blue van.

Ben thought he had prepared himself for seeing Ellie again, but when he came around the mill and caught sight of her, he felt uncustomarily ill at ease. It was too soon after the pain of the night before. He hesitated, reminding himself that he was there on sheriff's business. Assuming a matter-of-fact tone, he introduced Ellie to the other men—Leland Griffin, a deputy, and Dr. Briar, the county coroner. And as he watched her greet the men, he wanted to take her into his arms and pretend they hadn't left each other with a vast chasm between them.

Ellie turned to Ben. "Thank you for coming so quickly." Now that he was there, all her intentions of remaining calm and businesslike flew out of her head. She lost the remainder of what she had meant to say.

He looked down at her, his eyes gleaming with light mockery. "I always come quickly when somebody says they've found a body."

He was so relaxed as he walked over to the hole in the foundation that Ellie began to wonder if she'd made more of last night than he'd intended. Had he really said he loved her?

The doctor and the deputy moved to stand on either side of Ben.

"Why, it's just a child," Dr. Briar said in surprise.

Ben looked over his shoulder at Ellie and she had to look away for a moment to gather her wits. Then she said, "I didn't take time to explain anything on the phone. I just thought the sooner you got here, the better."

"We think it's William Swafford," Jake put in.

"Has to be," Pearl added. "He's the only child that's disappeared from these parts for as long as I can remember."

"How old was the Swafford boy, Ben, when he disappeared?" the doctor asked.

"Two."

Dr. Briar bent to study the skeleton more closely. "It's about the right size."

"Yeah, and William's been gone three years," the

deputy said, "time enough for the flesh to have deterio-rated."

Ben was looking at Ellie searchingly. "What prompted you to dig into the foundation?"

"Somebody was coming here at night and trying to get these stones loose. I kept hearing noises."

Ben ducked his head, looking almost embarrassed. "I remember."

"This morning I noticed that he'd been at it again while we—" She flushed enough so that Pearl looked sideways at her questioningly. Ellie tried to regroup. "While I was gone. There were a lot more mortar scrapings on the ground than there had been before. Obviously there was something in there that somebody wanted. So we made that hole."

"She thought Jimmy Gunter was doing it," Jake provided helpfully.

Ellie said defensively, "I remembered that the things Jimmy and his friends stole from the high school had never been found. I started to wonder if he could have hidden them in the foundation when he was helping Oliver Hilderbrand work on the mill."

"I should've told you," Ben said. "Jimmy decided to take Hilderbrand's advice. He came in to see me Friday and made a clean breast of everything. They sold the stolen goods at a pawn shop in Rogers. I called the shop and we'll be able to recover most of it. And now that Jimmy's cooperating, the judge has agreed to proba-tion."

"Oh." Ellie shrugged. "That's good." She couldn't think of anything else to say with Ben watching her so closely. When he turned away to tell the deputy to bring the stretcher from the van, Ellie suddenly thought: So it wasn't Jimmy Gunter. Then who was it?

She watched the men carefully remove the skeleton from its hiding place and place it on the stretcher. Ben covered it with a thin blanket. "You go on to town with Doc," he said to the deputy. "I'm going to look around here before I come back."

The doctor and Griffin disappeared around the corner of the mill with the stretcher, and the Vinings went into the mill. Without further comment, Ben walked toward the woods.

"Ben . . ." Ellie called after him. What she wanted to do was beg him to stop treating her with such casualness, but that would only make matters worse. "I'd like to go with you."

He didn't turn around for a moment, and she could sense refusal and rushed on, "Couldn't we talk, Ben? There's so much you don't understand, so much I want to say."

"Ellie, I'm working now," he said quietly.

The rebuff hurt dreadfully. "I'll help you." Before he could refuse, she had reached his side.

Her first impulse, he noted, had been to retreat. It hadn't been easy for her to come to him instead. Hadn't he known from the beginning that he would need patience in dealing with Ellie? "All right, come along."

He heard her small expulsion of breath. "Thank you."

He thrust his hands into his pockets and walked deeper into the trees, his gaze sweeping the ground.

Ellie watched him for a moment, feeling hurt. Evidently he didn't want to talk about them, not now. She had inflicted more pain than she'd realized. Sighing, she ran a few steps to keep up with him. "What are we looking for?"

"I don't know. Whoever has been digging at your foundation has to get here somehow. If he came through the woods, he might have left some evidence behind."

Ellie felt a little chill, even though she was wearing her jacket and it wasn't a cold day. "Do you think he knows what was in there?"

He bent to examine a small clearing in the trees more closely. "Why else was he trying to get inside?"

She kicked at some leaves. "It just doesn't add up. If it's William Swafford, he's been there for three years. If somebody knew where he was, why didn't they get him out in time to do him some good?"

Ben straightened. "Maybe he was already dead when he was left there."

This was a thought that Ellie had been trying not to entertain. "Nobody would have done that, unless—"

"Unless they'd killed him? Yes."

"Oh, Ben." Ellie shivered and hunched her shoulders in her jacket. "You don't think William could have fallen into the foundation and been unable to get out?"

"He was two years old, Ellie. Two-year-olds walk and climb everywhere. If he'd fallen in, he'd have been able to use the rough stone surface to climb out."

"Unless he knocked himself unconscious when he fell," she suggested, not very convincingly.

"I suppose that's possible." She could tell he didn't think the possibility was very strong. "But why didn't he crawl out when he regained consciousness?"

She looked into his concerned eyes. "He would have, I guess."

They walked on. After a while, Ellie said, "It still doesn't make sense. Suppose somebody did kill William and put his body in the foundation and piled rocks on top of it. The body was well hidden. By the time Oliver started rebuilding the mill, there was nothing but bone left. Obviously Oliver didn't discover it—he built the wall on top of it and left it there. Now, all of a sudden, three years later, somebody—I suppose whoever put it there—wants to get it out. Just since I moved into the mill. Why, Ben? I would never have discovered the body if they hadn't kept damaging the foundation."

"I don't have all the answers, Ellie. Wait, move back a step. What's that?"

He dropped to his hands and knees and thrust his arm to the shoulder under a thick, scratchy growth of tight underbrush. "I thought I saw something. There is something here." He dragged out a brown leather sandal, much the worse for wear and weather. Dropping the sandal, he reached again and brought out its mate. Then he pulled out a roll of what appeared to be clothing. Clearly the bundle had been wet through several times by rain, and the outer layer was an indistinguishable color.

Ben shook out the bundle. A pair of faded jeans wrapped around a red knit shirt.

"Maybe they were Mandy's," Ellie suggested. But

why were they hidden in the woods? Unaccountably, apprehension quivered through her and she took a step toward Ben.

He could hear the nervousness in her voice, and although he had promised himself not to risk touching her, she looked so bewildered that he couldn't resist putting his arm around her and drawing her close to him. "Don't be frightened. Maybe they *were* Mandy's. Maybe she decided to go skinny dipping in the creek and left them here, meaning to come back for them later, but forgot. I'll take these back to town with me." He wanted to kiss her, but things were so different since last night. He wasn't sure that she would welcome his kiss.

For a single sweet moment, Ellie let her head touch his shoulder, smelled his smell, felt his strength. Then, shaking off the daze, she stepped out of the curve of his arm. "Ben, about last night . . . I hurt so badly after you'd gone. I do care for you—very much. Don't lose patience with me, please."

He drew a deep, unsteady breath. "I'm trying to understand, Ellie." They walked back toward the mill, not touching.

At the edge of the woods she glanced over at him. His look was level, deep. "I have to get these to the lab," he said. "Would it be all right if I stopped by on my way home this evening?"

He saw surprise in her eyes, and then pleasure. She smiled. "Yes, I'll be waiting."

She had just closed the mill for the day and was climbing the stairs when the telephone rang. Assuming it was Ben, she dashed the rest of the way into her bedroom and grabbed the instrument on its fourth ring.

"Hello."

"Ellie? You sound out of breath." It was Liz. She stifled her disappointment.

"I just ran upstairs. It's good to hear from you. I gave up trying to find you at home."

"I haven't been home much the past month. We've been so busy making plans . . . I'm getting married!"

"To Hank, I presume. Congratulations, Liz."

Ellie knew that Liz had to be smiling in her dazzling way. She sounded so pleased. "Oh, Ellie, I've never been so happy! I won't say that I haven't wished for a little more time to get used to it. But Hank has to get back to work and he doesn't want to go without me. So I have to decide what to do about the shop. I think I'll try to find somebody to lease it for the time being. You aren't disillusioned with the gristmill business, are you?"

"No," Ellie answered, barely managing to wedge the word in.

"Ah, I didn't think so. Well, I'll work out something about the shop. I'd like to open one in Wichita or wherever we end up, and I'll have to sell this one eventually in order to buy another. I don't want Hank subsidizing me. I've made that clear. My business life is my own, and it'll remain that way. We've decided on November fifth. Just a small ceremony with the immediate families and a few friends. I'd be honored if you'd handle the guest book. Could you?"

Ellie sat down on the side of the bed. "Yes," she murmured faintly.

"Great! I knew you would. I've found the most fabulous dress. Ecru lace. Wait till you see it! I'm having only one attendant, my sister. And Hank's brother will be best man. We're getting married in his great-aunt's house, a wonderful old Victorian. Mums in all the Ozark autumn colors . . . I want them everywhere."

Ellie listened as Liz rattled on about her wedding plans. Liz was often animated, but love had made her frenetic. Eventually she wound down and Ellie said, "It sounds lovely. I'm so happy for you, Liz."

"You don't sound too happy," Liz said, "and come to think of it, neither did Ben when I told him earlier today."

"Liz, I—"

"No, now let me finish. Ben and I have had a couple of talks recently. Don't be upset. We're old friends and I've always told him my troubles. It's only fair that I listen to his. He didn't expect to fall in love with you, and he doesn't know quite what to do about it. I advised him to tell you how he felt."

"He did tell me. Last night."

"Oh, Ellie." Liz sounded slightly subdued for the first time during the conversation. "He didn't tell me, really he didn't, or I wouldn't have mentioned it. I take it things didn't go well. Otherwise, you'd both be happier today."

Ellie wound the phone cord around her finger. "I disappointed him, I'm afraid," she said helplessly.

"Now, Ellie, Ben's told me that you had a difficult time in your marriage. He didn't say anything more specific than that. I don't mean to upset you. We all have our problems, and we learn to cope. Even though I'm sure at the time you doubted you'd ever trust another man again."

"No," Ellie murmured. "No, I was sure I wouldn't."

"But you've let Ben into your life, little by little. You both deserve some happiness, and you're a giving woman. It'll work out, dear."

Perhaps it was Liz's well-meaning desire for everyone she knew to be as happy as she was, perhaps the privacy provided by the fact that Liz was nine miles away, that caused Ellie to reveal more than she would have in other circumstances.

"When Greg told me he wanted a divorce, I wanted to die. I'd tried so hard to be what he wanted in a wife. After nine years, I'd forgotten that I had ever wanted anything different, that I'd ever been a whole person on my own. I felt so lost and there was nobody I could turn to. My mother . . ." She drew a long breath. "My mother and I have never been close, and she wasn't very sympathetic. Perhaps she thought sympathy wasn't what I needed. She handled my father's death with such . . . such competence. No use crying over spilled milk. I remember her saying that. I was only ten years old at the time, and I wanted to attack her for sounding so casual about my father's death. And when I was hurting about Greg I wanted to cry and scream and have somebody tell me it was a natural reaction. Mother said I was weak, that if I wanted to be encouraged in my self-pity, I'd called the wrong person."

"Bull," Liz said rudely. "A little self-pity never hurt

anyone, especially if there's good reason for feeling sorry for yourself. And tears are therapy, a natural step in living through grief. It's the stoic ones who bottle it up inside who have problems later."

Ellie laughed. "If I'd had you in Houston, I wouldn't have needed to pay a counselor."

"From what I've seen, you've been able to put it behind you. You're here now, and you have Ben."

"I'm not so sure I do." Ellie lay back on the bed, feeling drained after her impulsive confidence. "With Ben, it has to be total commitment."

"He'll make a wonderful husband, Ellie."

"I'm not ready to marry again. I'm not sure I'll ever be."

"Ever?" Liz inquired disbelievingly. "Oh, ever is a terribly long time. Of course, you'll marry again. You don't want to live the rest of your life alone."

"Yes, but . . ." Ellie frowned, too tired to argue with any conviction.

"Ben's just pushing you a little too fast. It's just like him."

"Last night, I may have botched things beyond repair. He didn't ask me to marry him in so many words, but he made it clear he won't settle for less. And I'm afraid I made it clear the idea scared me to death."

"He's afraid of losing you. He does love you dreadfully."

"He has agreed to talk about it. Maybe I can make him understand how I feel."

Liz was silent a moment, "You know, if you love him, you'd be a fool to let him go. You'd hate yourself for the rest of your life. When Hank asked me to marry him, I started thinking of all the problems involved in leaving the shop and moving away from Springville, which I love, and the fact that it's all happened so fast. Hank made me realize that when happiness is offered you'd better grab it while you can. And hang on to it for dear life. If you never take any risks, you'll end up with nothing. Don't think so much, Ellie. Act on your feelings."

Liz's words stayed in Ellie's mind as she fixed a snack for herself and did the laundry and waited for Ben. She had to make a decision. Ben wouldn't wait around forever. He had offered her all that he had to give, and now it was time she offered him something in return. If she didn't want to lose Ben, she would have to tell him how she felt about him.

She was so keyed up that when the telephone rang again, she jumped violently. It was Ben.

"I'm sorry, Ellie, but I'm not going to be able to get away as early as I'd hoped. Something's come up here. I'll have to stay."

She was all primed to open her heart to him, to risk being vulnerable, and his words disappointed her. "How late will you be?"

"No way of knowing. If it's not too late, I'll still stop at your place . . . if that's all right."

"Yes, that's fine." She felt so deflated that it must have shown in her voice.

"Ellie . . ."

"Yes?"

"If it weren't so important, I'd be there now. I want to see you."

"It's all right, Ben. I understand."

And she tried to. But the evening dragged by interminably, and she grew more and more restless, until her nerves were strung taut enough to snap. At eleven-thirty she gave up on Ben. He was working all night. He wasn't coming.

She went to bed. She thought of Ben until it became clear that she would never get to sleep that way. She thought of peaceful meadows and drowsing Ozark summer days, and finally she drifted off.

The sound of singing awakened her. She'd left the bedroom window open a crack, and a clear female voice floated to her on the cool breeze. She got up and, without turning on a light, looked out the window. The moon was full and the old bridge spanning Wildhorse Creek was a black outline against the deep gray background of trees and sky. The singing continued.

> *"Mother, Mother, make my bed*
> *Make it long and narrow.*
> *Sweet William died for me last night.*
> *I'll die for him tomorrow."*

Like Pearl, Ellie had come to think of it as Mandy's song. Frightened, she huddled at the window, trying to detect exactly where the voice was coming from. It seemed to be coming from the bridge, but she saw no one.

As the minutes passed, Ellie's fright began to turn to anger. Pearl had been wrong. The removal of the child's skeleton hadn't satisfied whoever was out there. They meant to keep on harrassing her, frightening her. Who was doing this to her?

It had to stop. She was fed up with being terrorized in her own home. No more. She had to put a stop to it right now.

Moving in the dark, she felt through her closet until her hand found the velour of her heavy robe. She put it on along with a pair of leather house slippers.

Feeling her way so that she wouldn't run into something and make a noise, she moved carefully to the bedside table and slid open its drawer. Her fingers closed over the gun.

It was eerie going down the stairs in the dark, but she couldn't risk turning on a light. With excruciating care, she unlocked the front door, turned the knob, and inched the door open just far enough to slip through sideways.

At the bottom of the steps, she halted to listen. The singing had stopped.

The gun was cold in Ellie's hand as she crept around the mill house and halted for a few moments to allow her eyes to grow accustomed to the dark. Finally she made her way toward the bridge. Twice, she checked the safety catch, making sure she knew how to release it. She might not be able to shoot the singer, but she could fire high to frighten her.

The silence was unnerving as Ellie neared the bridge. Where was she? Had she seen Ellie and run away? Or was she watching silently from the shadows? Prickles of apprehension ran up and down Ellie's spine. She concentrated on the gun in her hand, to give herself courage. She had come this far. She had to go on with it.

Ellie stepped onto the bridge.

Chapter Fourteen

Sweet William died for me last night . . ."

The singing had resumed. The song was much clearer than it had been from the mill house. It came from the woods on the opposite side of the creek. Ellie grew still, gripping the bridge railing. She was terrified, but she had to face whatever was in the woods if she was ever to have peace. Holding the pistol in front of her at waist level, she started across the bridge.

Its span seemed to stretch for a very long way in front of her. She felt exposed, vulnerable on the bridge. She gripped the pistol handle so tightly that her hand hurt. She moved her shoulders, trying to relax taut muscles, and kept walking.

The song ended, and the silence slid back stealthily to embrace the bridge and Ellie. She pushed her hair away from her face and found her forehead damp with the sweat of fear. Halfway across the bridge, she was seized by a feeling of being followed. A drop of perspiration trickled between her breasts. She whirled around, clutching at a metal bridge brace with her free hand.

There was nothing behind her that human eyes could see. Straining forward, she tried to peer beyond the bridge to the encircling woods, but the trees appeared to be a solid blackness with no discernible breaks.

Nerves. She took deep breaths of the chill night air, steadying herself, and let her gaze sweep the woods once more. Nothing. Perhaps the singer had gone away. She would, she decided, go on to the far side of the bridge, where she had last heard the singing, before she turned back.

She heard a faint, whispering rustle as of a silk gown swaying against the legs of its wearer. The sound came from behind her, and as she half turned, her terror increased tenfold. A white specter rose up off the bridge and leapt toward her. Two white hands clamped on her shoulders, bearing her down, and the gun flew out of Ellie's hand and thudded on the bridge.

The specter was behind her, pushing. Ellie frantically grabbed those ghostly wrists. They felt solid. She tried to push them away, to break the specter's hold, but she was off-balance and couldn't manage it.

A knee wedged against her back, and belatedly Ellie realized it had been a mistake to let go of the bridge brace. She reached for it, her fingers grappling for the solid metal, but it was too late. She was shoved mightily from behind and lost her footing. She cried out. In a slow arc, her body toppled over the low bridge railing and tumbled into the water.

She plunged beneath the surface of the water and came up, flailing. For an instant, the cold shock of it took her breath away. Then her breath rushed out of her in a shudder of panic. Still flailing, she tried to orient herself. Somehow the moonlight had been taken away, and she was in near-total darkness. Treading water, she turned in a circle and saw that the moonlight still reflected in the water several hundred yards ahead of her. She was beneath the bridge, shrouded in the blackness of its shadow.

She shook with cold and wondered if the woman who had pushed her was still on the bridge, trying to find Ellie in the water. She heard nothing, but she stayed in the shadows, treading water, not knowing which way to swim to try to get out. She couldn't stay there long. It was too cold and her energy was being used up with shaking.

She was still there in the darkness in an agony of indecision when the paddle wheel creaked and began to move sluggishly through the water. Every nerve in Ellie's body jerked to attention. The wheel picked up speed, the noise shattered the silence. The bridge vibrated above her and the water rushed past in a swift current created by the movement of the wheel.

It was a few moments before she realized that she was being drawn inexorably toward the wheel with the current. A few more yards and she would come out of the shadows into the moonlight. Gathering what was left of her strength, Ellie lunged sideways toward one of the heavy bridge supports. Her arms encircled the support as her chest banged painfully against it. For a moment the breath was knocked out of her, but she held on and gasped frantically for oxygen. Her chest muscles finally admitted air, it seared painfully. Her chest heaved, and she clutched the bridge support, the vibrations from the wheel rattling through her body, and waited for her breathing to return to a semblance of normality.

Slowly her brain began to emerge from the cloud of panic and she could think again. Whoever had pushed her had gone inside the mill and turned on the paddle wheel. After having the lock changed, Ellie had left the door standing open! At long last, perhaps too late, it dawned on Ellie that whoever had been harrassing her was no longer trying merely to frighten her. The woman wanted to kill her. She would be out there somewhere, waiting for Ellie's body to be caught and battered by the paddle wheel. What would she do when she realized it wasn't going to happen?

She must have the gun now.

God, Ellie, think!

Could she make the woman believe that her murderous plan had worked? It was worth a try. Clinging to the support with first one hand and then the other, Ellie peeled off her soggy velour robe. With her free hand, she pushed the robe away from her until the current caught it. In the moonlight, the pink velour was pale against the blackness of the water. It whirled and tumbled in the current and, within seconds, was snagged by one of the huge paddles. The noise the wheel made changed subtly for a moment, became more labored, as the paddles chewed at the robe.

Ellie waited in the safe darkness beneath the bridge. Had the woman seen the robe? Had she been fooled? Was she convinced that Ellie was now dead, beaten beyond recognition by the wheel?

Ellie waited as long as she could, chills wracking her body. She couldn't stay in the cold water indefinitely. She barely had the strength left to swim out. It took every ounce of courage she possessed to let go of the solid security of the bridge support.

She pushed away from it, toward the opposite side of the bridge from the wheel, away from the treacherous current. Heaving through the water with all her might, holding back nothing, her system flooded with adrenalin, she swam toward the bank.

Never before had she been so aware of the fact that time is relative. The minutes required to reach the bank seemed like hours. But finally she was climbing out, her hands and feet finding solid ground at last.

Barefoot and shivering in her wet nightgown, she wrapped her arms around herself for whatever warmth they could give and walked back across the bridge. Cautiously, she made her way over the rough, grassy ground toward the mill house.

Ellie rounded a corner and stopped in her tracks. She was face to face with the white-gowned specter who had pushed her from the bridge. Ellie's heart crashed against her ribs. Everything about the woman in white was pale and insubstantial, dress, face, and long, flowing hair. For an instant Ellie imagined that she could almost see through her. But after that one fleeting instant, she managed to get a grip on her imagination.

The woman had gone stock-still at the sight of Ellie. She was as shocked by the confrontation as Ellie was, and while Ellie was still trying to decide whether to run or use the moment of surprise in some other way to her own advantage, the woman spoke.

"You're dead. Stay away from me. I saw you go under the wheel. You're dead!" Her voice was shrill, wild.

Ellie didn't dare to move or speak, for fear of dispelling the woman's delusion. As long as she thought she was confronting a ghost, she wouldn't attack Ellie again. So Ellie just stood there, shivering, her teeth clamped together to keep them from chattering. And tried to figure out how she could get around the woman and run for the front door of the mill house.

"You stole my home," the woman accused, "and now you've taken William away."

She was young. That much Ellie could tell in the moonlight. But what did she mean by her home? Was she talking about the mill?

"Where did you put my baby brother?"

"Mandy?" Unconsciously, Ellie took a step toward her.

The woman shrank back, and the hand she had kept behind her until now came out, holding a gun. The pistol Ellie had dropped on the bridge. "Stay away from me!"

It was Mandy. It had to be. She wasn't a ghost. And her face was unmarred. But Jake and Oliver and Ben had seen her dead, her face battered to pulp. All of these thoughts crowded into Ellie's mind at once, but she couldn't think about any of that now. She shoved them aside and concentrated on getting out of this alive.

"I won't hurt you, Mandy," Ellie said, hoping the woman was so frightened she wouldn't notice the terrified tremor in Ellie's voice. "And you might as well drop that gun. It can't hurt me."

"You moved William," Mandy murmured. The gun wavered in her hand, but she didn't drop it. "I fixed him a nice, warm place and covered him up with rocks where I could keep him company and sing to him. Then you came, and I tried to dig him out. I wanted to take him away and hide him again. You had no right to move him."

Ellie watched the lowered gun from the corner of her eye. "What happened, Mandy? How did William die?"

She whimpered suddenly, like a small, frightened child. "I didn't mean to." She glanced around frantically as though she were unable to focus her eyes, all at once. Then her gaze came back to Ellie and she held her head to one side in an expression of surprise as if she were seeing Ellie for the first time. Mandy Hilderbrand was quite mad. The certainty sent a fresh shock of fear through Ellie.

Her voice rigidly controlled, Ellie soothed, "I know, Mandy. I know you didn't mean to."

"Do you?" Mandy asked wistfully.

"Yes."

"He came after me, you see."

"Who?"

"The truant officer. Always snooping around, saying I had to go to school or he'd send me away, make me live with people I didn't know who'd see I went to school. He came to the cabin and I grabbed William and ran to the woods. He came after us, yelling. We hid in the foundation. I heard him crashing through the woods, coming to the mill. William started to cry. I put my hand over his mouth and held him tight against me. I only meant to keep him quiet. When the truant officer went away, I let William go. He wouldn't move. I shook him and slapped him, but he wouldn't move. I covered him up and left him there. Everybody looked for him—for days. But they didn't find him. I felt so sad and, finally, I told Pa what had happened." She halted and, lowering her head, brought the gun closer to her face. She acted as if she didn't know how it had gotten into her hand. Then she looked up. "Pa was drinking moonshine. He hit me and said I lied."

Ellie hardly dared to breathe, but Mandy seemed to expect some response. "About William?"

"Yes. He said I killed William on purpose. He said I was bad and crazy and he was going to have me locked up. He tried to catch me, but I ran away. He came after me. Over there—" she gestured vaguely with the gun in her hand—"near the cave, he fell and knocked himself out cold. He didn't get up." She had begun to sway slightly as she talked. Behind her, pale light penetrated the darkness at the front corner of the mill house.

Ellie heard the muffled sound of an engine. Car lights. Someone was coming! She had to distract Mandy. "It wasn't your fault, Mandy." The light grew brighter, the sound of the engine louder.

"I knew there was a nest of rattlers in that cave," Mandy said slyly. "I left Pa there. He shouldn't have said he'd have me locked up."

"No, he shouldn't have done that," Ellie agreed, and heard the car stop in front of the mill house. The motor was turned off, the car door slammed. Let it be Ben, she prayed.

The slam of the car door jerked Mandy's head around. Her long, blond hair flew around her like a cape.

Ellie heard someone climbing the front steps. Let it be Ben. "It's my friend," she said soothingly. "He won't hurt you." She raised her voice. "Ben?"

"Ellie?" He clambered down the front steps and strode around the corner of the mill house. His eyes hadn't yet become fully accustomed to the darkness. He made out two figures, nothing more. "Ellie? What's going on?"

Mandy bolted. As fleet and swift as a deer, she disappeared into the woods.

Ellie swayed on her feet. Too much had happened. She was sure she was going to faint. She fought off the dizziness and found her voice. "Oh, God, Ben . . . thank goodness you came." She stumbled forward and fell into his arms.

His arms tightened around her, and for a moment she gave in to the swirl of blackness that threatened to envelop her. Her eyes closed, she buried her face in Ben's jacket and clung to him.

"You're wet!" He lifted her in his arms and carried her into the mill house. "My God, sweetheart, what happened?"

"You came. Oh, Ben, I'm so glad you came," she murmured as he carried her up the stairs.

"There weren't any lights on." He flipped switches as

he entered the apartment, flooding the rooms with light. "I wasn't going to stop, but then I saw the front door standing open." He set her down in the bedroom. "Take that wet gown off. I'll get a towel."

He went into the bathroom, taking his warmth with him. Shivering, Ellie pulled the gown over her head, then stepped out of her wet panties. Ben came back with a big towel and rubbed it briskly over her, then wrapped it around her. He handed her the smaller towel he'd brought for her hair.

She sat on the side of the bed and made a turban of the towel. He was looking at her in a calm, steady way. She didn't lower her eyes when he looked into hers. Without speaking, he sat beside her and gathered her close and held her. With a sigh, she clung to him and felt her tension easing.

The strength of his arms made her feel safe. "Oh, Ben, Mandy tried to kill me. She didn't die. I don't understand how you all could have thought—"

"It was Anne Brohaugh who died."

She lifted her head and the towel turban came loose and slipped down her back. "Who?"

Ben brushed a wayward lock of hair out of her eyes. "I think I mentioned to you once that a Tulsa man had come into the office looking for his sixteen-year-old daughter. She'd run away." Ellie nodded and he went on, "Later he sent me a picture of Anne, but I didn't put it together until I found those clothes hidden in the woods this morning. When I left here, I went back to the office to check the description of Anne Brohaugh that her father had sent me. She was wearing jeans, a knit shirt, and sandals when she disappeared. She was about Mandy's size and had long, blond hair. I finally tracked Brohaugh down in Oklahoma City, where he'd gone on business, and he drove to Springville to identify the clothing. I had to wait for him at the office. After he'd made the I.D., he wanted to talk about his daughter and we went to an all-night restaurant. That's why I was so late getting here."

Ellie shook her head, trying to assimilate what he was telling her. "Does he know that his daughter is dead?"

"I couldn't tell him," Ben admitted. "I still had a few doubts myself until I got here and found you with her."

"You saw Mandy, then?"

"Briefly, before she ran into the woods. I knew that's who it had to be, although I'd never seen her before."

"That explains why you didn't realize it wasn't Mandy who died under the mill wheel, but what about Jake and Oliver?"

"You know how bad Jake's eyesight is. All he saw was blond hair and a white dress. After they got the body out, Hilderbrand carried it upstairs and later that day he buried it. Jake didn't see it again. Doc Briar saw the body briefly—a requirement for the death certificate—but he'd never seen Mandy before, either."

"But according to Jake," Ellie murmured, "Oliver said, 'Mandy, Mandy, what have you done?' as though he believed it was Mandy, that she'd committed suicide."

"There's another interpretation that can be put on Hilderbrand's words. If he thought Mandy had pushed Anne into the creek . . ."

Ellie's eyes widened as certainty settled over her. Ben was right. Mandy had killed Anne Brohaugh, and Oliver knew it. Oliver, whom she had defended and trusted.

"A deputy is supposed to be at my place tomorrow morning at eight. We were going after the Hilderbrands. But after what's happened tonight, I'll have to go now. It isn't safe to let Mandy run loose another hour."

She had known what he would say, even before he said it. He had no other choice. "I'm going with you."

"Ellie." He wanted her safely locked inside the mill house until Mandy was no longer a threat to her.

"Don't say no, Ben. Please. I'll feel safer with you than I would here alone. The gun you gave me—I dropped it, and Mandy has it now." She saw the alarm in his eyes quickly smothered. She stood and went to the bureau, pulled out jeans and a sweatshirt, then headed for the bathroom.

"We'll have to walk most of the way. It's five miles to their cabin."

At the bathroom door she turned back to say, "I'll be ready in five minutes."

In fact, it was only four minutes later when they stepped out of the mill house, locking the door behind them. At the bottom of the steps, Ben suddenly turned her to him and kissed her with heat and feeling. Lifting his head, he muttered, "You stay close to me. I don't want anything to happen to you."

They drove in Ben's car about a half mile along a road to a spot that Ben said was a little closer to the Hilderbrand cabin. He stopped the car, checked his holstered pistol, and took a flashlight from the glove compartment. "We walk from here."

The path was wide enough for them to walk abreast. Ben took her hand and led the way, the flashlight beam picking out the twists of the path in front of them.

Bundled in jeans, sweatshirt, and a lined jacket, Ellie was warm enough. The shivers that ran through her now and then came from tension. She said softly, "Mandy's insane, Ben. There's no telling what she might do."

He squeezed her hand. "I'd already come to that conclusion on my own."

"She killed her brother. She admitted it to me. They were hiding from a truant officer, and in trying to keep him quiet, she smothered him. When she told her father what she'd done, he threatened to have her locked up. He chased her through the woods. He was drunk, and he fell and knocked himself unconscious near a den of rattlesnakes. Mandy knew the danger, but she left him there."

Ben looked down at her curiously. "You two had quite a chat."

"She thought I was a ghost."

He chuckled and tucked her hand into his jacket pocket. "Maybe we'd better not talk," he cautioned. "We'll scare her off if she's still around here."

They walked in silence for several minutes. Then Ben stopped abruptly. "Listen," he whispered.

The faint sound of singing drifted to them through the trees. "This way," Ben said and headed into the trees on their right. There wasn't room to walk beside him, and Ellie followed at his heels. They walked for a good long while before Ben stopped. Ahead of them, in a clearing, a white figure swayed beneath the moon, singing of William's death.

Ellie whispered urgently, "She's standing next to the cliff."

"She's still got the gun," Ben whispered. They watched Mandy for several moments as she continued to sway and sing. Finally, Ben said, "Well, I have to do something. Move away from me, Ellie."

Alarm sliced through her. "What are you going to do?"

"Don't make me sorry I brought you. Do as I say!"

Ellie moved to one side, away from him, her heart in her throat, fear for Ben a knot in her stomach.

Ben moved to the edge of the clearing, just within the shelter of the trees. He called out, "Mandy?"

The singing stopped. Mandy froze and darted looks about her in every direction. "Who are you?"

"A friend, Mandy. I want to help you. Throw down your gun and—No! Watch out for the cliff, Mandy!"

Ben ran forward, but before he could reach Mandy, she had backed to the edge of the cliff, and as Ellie watched, horrified, she took another step back into space and hurtled down. Her scream of terror split the air.

Ellie ran from her hiding place to Ben's side. "I'm going down," Ben said. "There's a way. We found it when we had to bring that hunter out. You wait here." Before she could reply, he was running along the rim of the cliff and soon disappeared into the trees.

Ellie waited. She prayed for Ben's safety. There was plenty of time for praying, and for thinking. Because it turned her insides to a mass of nerves to think about Ben making the steep descent to Mandy, she thought about afterward, when this was all over and she and Ben could be alone and talk. The future was not as clear as Ellie would have liked it to be. When she had married Greg, she hadn't considered anything but a "happily ever after" ending. She'd been naive and inexperienced and full of young dreams. Now she was older and more cautious. She wanted to see clearly where she was going before she took the first step. Perhaps that was unrealistic. But when she told Ben she loved him, she wanted to be free of doubts. She couldn't offer him love with reservations.

And she didn't want to risk losing him, either. Beyond everything else, that was perfectly clear to her. She wanted to be able to expect him in the evenings, to talk to him, to share things with him. Her life would be pointless without that now. He'd become essential to her happiness.

She remembered how his touch made her feel, and she trembled with need. A mere look from him across a room could turn her liquid inside. With Ben, she felt a contentment she'd never known before, just preparing a meal together or walking in the woods.

She couldn't imagine a future without him—didn't want to imagine it. Surely that was love. There would be risks, but she had to be willing to take chances again. She had to find the courage.

A shot rang out.

Ellie felt the cold shock of fear. "No!" Lying down, she edged to the rim of the cliff to look over. It was too dark to see anything below. "Ben!" Her voice quavered with panic.

There was no answer. Perhaps he was too far away to hear her. Mandy must have survived the fall and hung on to the pistol, or there would have been no need for anybody to discharge a gun. Who had pulled that trigger—Ben or Mandy?

Oh, God, Ben . . .

She began to weep. "Oh, please don't die. I love you. I need you." No doubts now. Not a single one. She felt as if she had been walking through gelatin for weeks and had finally set foot on solid ground. She was a whole woman again, alive and desperately in love. And it hurt. If she lost Ben now . . .

"Ellie?"

She edged away from the cliff and got up. A stooped figure came toward her from the woods. "Oliver, is that you?" Perhaps she should have been afraid of him, but her emotions were all tied up with worry for Ben.

"I heard a gunshot."

"I don't know what's happened, Oliver. Mandy was here. She fell off the cliff, and Ben went down to find her." *She's insane! I'll never forgive you, Oliver, if she's killed Ben!* she thought on a fresh surge of desperation. Ben! Liz's words came back to haunt her: When happiness is offered you'd better grab it while you can. Her heart twisted. She wanted to tell Ben how much she loved him, how he had given her back herself. She wanted another chance.

Oliver buried his face in his hands and sobbed. She moved to his side and put her arm around his slumped shoulders. She tried to keep her voice calm. "Do you know the way down, Oliver?"

After a moment he choked back his sobs. "I was only trying to protect her. She isn't responsible . . ."

"We have to get to them. Ben may be hurt."

Oliver pulled himself together, squaring his shoulders. "I know the way. Come with me."

Chapter Fifteen

The way was very steep. They had no flashlight, but the moonlight was bright enough to show them the descending path, yet not enough to reveal every stick and stone. It took all of Ellie's nerve to stay up with Oliver. Presumably, he was familiar with the path, but for a sixty-year-old he had amazing stamina.

After long minutes of silence, as they scrambled down the steep incline, Ellie's heart dreading what they would find below, Hilderbrand asked, "How long have you known that Mandy was alive?"

"I only found out tonight. She—she tried to kill me, Oliver. She pushed me into the creek and turned on the paddle wheel."

He made a gutteral sound, as though he was in great

pain. "It's my fault. I should have had her committed after what she did to that poor child."

"Anne Brohaugh?"

He chanced a quick glance over his shoulder. "You know who she was then. Poor little girl. She'd run away from home. One day she turned up at the mill exhausted and hungry. I took her in. What else could I do? I fed her and told her to take a bath. Her clothes were filthy. I gave her one of Mandy's dresses to wear. I said she could stay with us until she decided what she was going to do. Jake was home, sick. There was no one there but Mandy and me. And Anne stayed out of the way, so none of the customers ever saw her. I thought I was helping her. I didn't dream Mandy would react the way she did."

"She was jealous?"

"She was beside herself. But I couldn't turn that child out. I told Mandy we'd have to let her stay until I could talk her into going back home. I think Anne would have called her parents and asked them to come after her, if I'd had more time to talk to her. You must believe me, Ellie. It never occurred to me that Mandy would harm her. But when Jake discovered the body that morning—his first day back at work after his illness—and told me it was Mandy, I knew even before I went outside what had happened. The girl was wearing Mandy's dress. I suppose, in Mandy's mind, that merely added insult to injury." They stumbled along in silence for a few moments. Then Oliver went on, "Somehow Mandy lured Anne outside that morning before I was awake and pushed her from the bridge.

Mandy ran off and hid in the woods, the way she always does when things become too much for her." He paused to draw a deep breath which he expelled with a sigh. "Since Anne's face was battered beyond recognition and everyone assumed it was Mandy, I let them go on thinking it. I couldn't bring myself to betray Mandy. Don't you see, I was to blame for showing Anne so much attention that Mandy felt threatened. Later, I found Mandy cowering behind a bush in the woods like a wounded animal."

"So you buried Anne Brohaugh in Mandy's grave."

"Yes," he muttered desolately. There was no plea for understanding in his tone, merely a deep regret.

"Did you know that Mandy is responsible for the deaths of her brother and father, as well?"

"I didn't know until after we'd buried Anne. Mandy doesn't understand the seriousness of what she's done, Ellie. She can't be held accountable. She told me about her brother and father when we moved out of the mill. That's when I finally admitted to myself how psychotic she really was." His voice broke, and after a moment he cleared his throat and said sadly, "There was absolutely no remorse. All Mandy was worried about was leaving William behind. It was all I could do to convince her we had to leave, that if anyone saw her they'd take her away from me and lock her up. I thought I could keep her protected in the cabin. I convinced myself that nobody would ever find out. But Mandy couldn't accept the idea of somebody else living in the mill house. I tried to keep her away from the mill, but she'd slip out of the house at night after I was asleep. Months ago, I lost one of the keys to the mill house. Mandy found it and she's been using it to get into the mill."

He was talking more to himself than to her now, Ellie realized. She might have felt more sympathy with him if she hadn't been so sick with worry over Ben. Oliver talked on, about Mandy, about his false perception of her in the beginning and his growing horror as he began to realize that she was insane. Ellie, intent upon keeping her footing, only half listened.

When the ground began to level out, Ellie whispered, "Oliver, maybe we'd better stop talking."

"I'm sorry. You're right," he responded.

Neither of them voiced the fear that if it had been Mandy who had fired the shot they heard earlier, she just might decide to shoot at them next. Neither of them had to.

They advanced as quietly as possible, which wasn't quiet at all. Leaves crackled underfoot and occasionally a dislodged pebble skittered into the darkness. The path grew steep again and finally wound to their right and they saw, below them, a frail beam of light. Hilderbrand held his arm out to warn her. They stopped.

After a moment Hilderbrand whispered, "What's that?"

Suddenly Ellie knew, and fear rose in her throat. Everything that was important to her was down there, centered somehow in the pale stream of light. It was Ben's flashlight.

"Ben!" she cried, and forgetting danger, she began

to scramble down the remainder of the incline, sliding and slipping and screaming inside. Twice she fell to her knees and scraped her hands on stones, but she didn't feel it. Everything but her mind was numb. *She's killed you, my darling, my Ben! It isn't fair!*

He was lying on his side, one arm outstretched, the flashlight inches from his hand. Ellie's legs buckled and she went down on her knees beside him. She touched his face with trembling fingers.

"Ben!"

He groaned and tried to sit up. Thank God, he was alive! Ellie applied gentle pressure to his shoulders. "Lie still, darling. You're hurt. Did she shoot you?"

"Shoot . . . ?" He moved his head and mumbled a curse, his fingers going to his temple. "I fell down the damn hill, got a bump as big as an egg." He pushed her hands away and sat up. "Talk about a migraine."

Tears of relief ran down Ellie's face. "Are you all right?"

He gripped her arm and tried to stand up and groaned again. "I will be."

She took his hand in both of hers and brought it to her cheek. "I thought . . . oh, Ben, I was so afraid. We heard a shot."

"My gun," he said suddenly, reaching for the flashlight and cursing when the movement sent another pain knifing through his head. He moved the light in a half circle. "There it is." He brought the gun to his nose and sniffed. "It's been fired. It must have discharged when I fell. Clumsy idiot . . ."

Smiling through her tears, Ellie kissed him. She

wanted to cling to him, but she was afraid of causing him more pain. She sat back on her heels and gently brushed at the dirt on his face.

"Ellie," he muttered, and leaned over to return her kiss. But before their lips made contact, Hilderbrand finally reached them.

"Did you find Mandy, Ben?"

Ben lifted his head and, over Ellie's worried protests, got slowly to his feet. He swayed for a moment, then steadied himself. "She's over there, Hilderbrand." He directed the flashlight beyond them to the base of the cliff. A white figure lay on the ground, frighteningly lifeless.

Hilderbrand cried out and ran forward. Ben put his arms around Ellie and pulled her against him. "I saw her and took my eyes off the path. The next thing I knew I was falling," he murmured into her hair. "The way she's lying, I think her neck's broken."

Ellie shuddered and he held her tighter.

Hilderbrand was sobbing. "She's dead," he choked out. "Oh, Mandy . . . Mandy . . ."

Dawn came softly, cradling the mill house like a soothing mother after the terrors of the night. Ellie had napped for an hour on the couch. Now she made coffee in the kitchen, trying to be quiet and not wake Ben.

He had stubbornly insisted that he could make it back to the car carrying Mandy's body, after Ellie and Hilderbrand had found him. And he had, just barely. Then Ellie had driven to the mill house. Ben had called his deputy, an ambulance, and Dr. Briar, who confirmed what they already knew—Mandy's neck was broken; she had died instantly.

"She never knew a moment's pain," the doctor had told Oliver, and the distress lines in Oliver's forehead eased a little.

When they'd brought Mandy into the lighted mill house and laid her on the folded quilt brought quickly from upstairs, Ellie had her first good look at the girl who had tried to kill her. Her white dress was dirty and torn, and her long hair was tangled. But her pretty face was as innocent and unmarked as a child's. It was almost impossible to believe that she had been responsible for the deaths of three people. She looked at peace, and this seemed to comfort Oliver. There was none of the disillusioned cynic in his voice when he told Ellie, "She's all right now. Somebody's taking care of her."

Mandy's body had been transported by ambulance to the funeral home in Springville, and Leland Griffin, the deputy, had taken Oliver to town to get his statement recorded. Then Dr. Briar had examined Ben, prescribed pain pills, and ordered him to bed. After the doctor was gone, Ellie helped Ben, whose eyes were already heavy from the pills, out of his shirt and trousers and tucked him into her bed. Not wanting to disturb him, she had tried to sleep on the couch, without much success.

Her mind had been too full of everything that had happened for her to sleep. Finally, she had given it up as a lost cause. She had checked on Ben, who was still sleeping soundly, then dressed and started coffee.

While she waited for the coffee to perk, she roamed from window to window, looking out, as the sky lightened and another glorious autumn day arrived. Along with the sadness she felt for Mandy and Oliver, there was also a new feeling of lightness and freedom. The mill house was no longer haunted. And she had been given a second chance with Ben. This time, she meant to make the most of it.

She wandered back into the kitchen, saw that the percolator's red light was on, and poured herself a cup of coffee. She heard movement from the bedroom the moment before Ben called her name.

Leaving her coffee, she went in to him. He was sitting up in bed and his blue eyes smiled at her when she appeared in the doorway.

For a moment they merely watched each other. She saw his expression change as she came over to the bed. The bruise at his temple was darker than it had been a few hours earlier, but the swelling had gone down. Ellie tested his forehead with her hand. "Feeling better?"

He lifted her hand from his brow and pulled her down on the bed to sit beside him. "Much. Did you get any sleep at all?"

She laid her head on his shoulder. "A little. Coffee's made. Would you like some?"

"Not now." Both his arms came around her. He pressed a moist kiss on her brow. "Has Leland called?"

"No. Will Oliver be arrested?"

"For harboring a murderer? The judge will probably release him on his own recognizance. If it ever goes to trial, he'll get off with probation."

"I'm glad. I feel so sorry for him. He thought he was helping Mandy."

For a moment, Ben held her wordlessly.

"Ben?"

"Ummm?"

She paused to take a deep breath. "Last night when I heard that gunshot and I thought you'd been shot . . ." She lifted her head so that she could look into his eyes steadily, with every mask removed. "I can't describe what it did to me. I thought I'd lost you and it hurt so much. I've never hurt like that before."

His hands cradled her face. "Not even during the divorce?"

She shook her head. "Not even then."

He held her eyes with his, unwavering. "Why do you think that was?"

"Because I love you," she said simply, "more than I've ever loved anyone. And I hadn't told you, and I thought I might never have another chance. The regret —it was like a knife in my heart."

He urged her head closer with both hands and pressed his mouth to hers and tightened his hold. The first rays of the sun filtered through the window and touched them as their mouths lingered moistly, hungrily.

He drew away at last and she could see traces of wonder in his eyes as he looked at her. "Are you sure?" he demanded.

"I've never been more sure of anything in my life. Oh, darling, I'm so sorry about the other night. You caught me off guard. I thought I couldn't handle another commitment, and there you were letting me know that you wanted nothing less."

"You just sat there, looking unhappy. I thought I'd jumped to conclusions—that you didn't love me."

"I tried to convince myself I didn't," she admitted, smiling wistfully, "because I was scared. My marriage was a disaster. I didn't want another failure. But out there on that cliff, when I thought I'd lost you, I saw everything clearly for the first time. I knew I didn't want to live without you."

He dropped a quick, hot kiss on her mouth. "I want to marry you."

"You do? Uh . . ."

He lifted a brow. "What is that, a definite maybe?"

Briefly her mouth touched his. "It's a yes. It's just going to take a little time for me to get used to the idea."

"You've got it." He lay back against the pillows and drew her down with him. "But while you're getting used to the idea, we have an hour before the Vinings are due. Let's not waste it."

His kiss drugged her. She murmured a final, anxious question before drifting away with the sensuous tide. "Are you sure you're up to it?"

He chuckled wickedly, nuzzling her throat. "That's exactly what I am, love. Here, let me show you."

She laughed softly. "You're awful, Sheriff."

He rolled over and on top of her. "Yeah, but you love me, anyway."

"I do," she said solemnly and, wrapping her arms around his neck, parted her lips for his kiss.

Epilogue

The April sun was caressingly warm on Ellie's bare arms as she bent to snip a bouquet of yellow tulips for the dinner table. She paused midway down the bordering row of tulips to sit back on her heels and admire her garden. To the rosebushes that were there when she had married Ben three months earlier, she'd added tulips, daffodils, petunias, geraniums, tiger lilies, and azaleas, even laying the stones herself for the path that meandered among the flowers. She had placed ivy runners next to the house, and they were beginning to crawl up the log wall. At one end of the garden, a small white fountain splashed and a bird feeder swung from an eave. Ellie grinned, watching a robin and a cardinal, perched on the rim of the fountain, fussing over territorial rights.

She had spent the past two hours rooting out every weed and stray blade of grass from the garden, and her body ached with a pleasant tiredness. She only worked mornings at the mill now, having found a young couple to live in the second-floor apartment. They were being trained by the Vinings to take over when Jake retired in a couple of months, and Ellie was pleased with their enthusiasm for the business.

Bending to the tulips again, she added four more to her bouquet and, standing, brushed dirt from the knees of her jeans. With a sigh of the purest contentment, she gazed at the woods, which began at the edge of the yard, lavished now by the pink of redbuds and the white of dogwoods in bloom.

"Lovely." Ben's voice behind her startled her, and she quickly turned.

She held the bouquet out in front of her. "Yes, aren't they?"

"I was talking about you, not the tulips."

She smiled as she crossed the garden toward him.

He slipped his arms around her waist. "Aren't you home a little early?"

"It was a dull day at the courthouse. In fact, there wasn't much going on anywhere in Springville today. A few shop owners sprucing up their windows for the season. Dull." He nuzzled into her neck, finding the spot just below her earlobe where she dabbed her cologne.

"I'll remind you of that a month from now when you're complaining about the tourists."

He drew away to look at her. "You've got dirt on your nose." He took out his handkerchief and brushed at the tip of her nose. Her smooth ivory complexion was tinged with a rosy underglow that made her more beautiful to him than ever. Marriage agreed with her. He particularly loved seeing her in her garden. She had turned their yard into a seductive Eden, the flowers and plants overflowing into the house. He returned his handkerchief to his pocket and kissed the spot he had just cleaned. "I love you, Ellie."

She crossed her wrists behind his head, not touching him with her dirty hands. The tulips pressed their yellow petals against his hair. "That's nice. Because I adore you." She smiled sweetly and drew his head down until their mouths met.

Locked in the feel and fragrance of her, Ben's gentle pleasure quickly turned to heated passion. "Is Oliver coming to dinner?" he murmured. Oliver had become their close friend during the past six months.

"No. He came by earlier to tell me he has to fill in for somebody on the youth hotline tonight. Apparently, they'd like to have him every night, he's so good with the kids."

"Uh-huh." His lips brushed her neck.

Ellie sighed softly. "He said the lawyer should have the abstract ready soon. We can probably close the deal for the mill next week." Ellie had convinced him she wanted to empty her bank account to pay for the mill. She liked to feel that she could handle her business on her own.

"That's good." He nibbled at her earlobe.

"He brought English peas from his garden for our dinner." She drew his head back far enough so that her mouth could find his.

Moments later, he said, "Let's go inside," and they walked slowly, hands linked, toward the house.

The log house glowed with sunshine and wax and the special, loving touches Ellie had added, making it truly their home. And Ellie herself was the most special touch of all. Her presence—her laughter, the joy she brought to everything she touched—filled every room.

The scent of lemon oil mixed with the enticing smell of the hickory-smoked ham baking in the kitchen.

Ellie washed her hands at the kitchen sink, then arranged the tulips in a crystal vase and carried them into the dining room to set them in the center of the linen-covered table, between two yellow tapers in crystal holders. Lounging in the dining room doorway, Ben watched her with an adoring half smile.

"The good crystal, Ellie? And why are we eating in the dining room?"

"I just felt like making a fuss."

"Is there something special about today that I've forgotten?" He wrinkled his brow. "It's not our three-month anniversary, is it?"

Ellie smiled at him. "That was two weeks ago."

"I thought so." He came to her and drew her into his arms.

"We're having your favorite wine with dinner. I got a bottle of it when I was in town earlier."

"You take such good care of me." His desire, aroused in the garden, was still pushing at him. His need for her, far from blending into more sedate feelings since their marriage, seemed rather to increase. He slid his hands up under her shirt to stroke her back.

"Mmmm." She leaned against him contentedly. "As you do, of me."

He looked down into her eyes, and she saw the stirring desire and naked love. He tasted her lips slowly, as though he would never get enough of kissing her. "Can dinner wait for a while?"

"I should think so," she murmured. "Did you have something more interesting in mind?"

"Interesting," he chuckled, "does not begin to do justice to what I have in mind."

As one, they turned to walk toward the bedroom. His arm encircled her waist, her head rested on his shoulder.

"Tell me more," she invited.

A few minutes later, she lay on their bed, naked on the sunflower quilt Pearl had given them as a wedding present. Her auburn hair fanned out across the pillows, and her eyes were heavy with love and dreamy arousal. His body covered hers, warm and lean and strong with the strength of a man with his woman. He supported his upper body with his elbows on either side of her, and his hands threaded through her hair. He kissed her lingeringly, lifting his head after a few moments to ask lazily, "What else did you do in town today?"

Her fingertip traced the firm outline of his bottom lip. "I went to see that new young doctor."

Soft kisses feathered her cheek and jaw. "Dr. Roads?"

"Yes."

He lifted his head to look into her eyes and saw reflected there the deep and abiding love they shared and found too wondrous to ever take it for granted. "It was just a routine checkup, wasn't it—everything's all right?"

She gave him an artless smile. "Everything is wonderful. We're going to have a baby."

His eyes widened as he took it in and then became as misty as hers. "You humble me, my precious love," he murmured, unashamed of the unsteady timbre of his voice. "I didn't think I could be any happier."

EYE OF THE STORM

MAURA SEGER

A powerful
portrayal of
the events of
World War II in the
Pacific, *Eye of the Storm* is a riveting story of how love
triumphs over hatred. In this, the first of a three book
chronicle, Army nurse Maggie Lawrence meets Marine
Sgt. Anthony Gargano. Despite military regulations
against fraternization, they resolve to face together
whatever lies ahead.... Also known by her fans as
Laurel Winslow, Sara Jennings, Anne MacNeil and
Jenny Bates, Maura Seger, author of this searing novel,
was named by ROMANTIC TIMES as 1984's Most
Versatile Romance Author.

At your favorite bookstore in March.

Fall in love again for the first time every time you read a Silhouette Romance novel.

Take 4 books free—no strings attached.

Step into the world of Silhouette Romance, and experience love as thrilling as you always knew it could be. In each enchanting 192-page novel, you'll travel with lighthearted young heroines to lush, exotic lands where love and tender romance wait to carry you away.

Get 6 books each month before they are available anywhere else!
Act now and we'll send you four touching Silhouette Romance novels. They're our gift to introduce you to our convenient home subscription service. Every month, we'll send you six new Silhouette Romance books. Look them over for 15 days. If you keep them, pay just $11.70 for all six. Or return them at no charge.

We'll mail your books to you *two full months before they are available anywhere else.* Plus, with every shipment, you'll receive the Silhouette Books Newsletter absolutely free. *And Silhouette Romance is delivered free.*

Mail the coupon today to get your four free books—and more romance than you ever bargained for.

Silhouette Romance is a service mark and a registered trademark.

READERS' COMMENTS ON SILHOUETTE SPECIAL EDITIONS:

"I just finished reading the first six Silhouette Special Edition Books and I had to take the opportunity to write you and tell you how much I enjoyed them. I enjoyed all the authors in this series. Best wishes on your Silhouette Special Editions line and many thanks."

—B.H.*, Jackson, OH

"The Special Editions are really special and I enjoyed them very much! I am looking forward to next month's books."

—R.M.W.*, Melbourne, FL

"I've just finished reading four of your first six Special Editions and I enjoyed them very much. I like the more sensual detail and longer stories. I will look forward each month to your new Special Editions."

—L.S.*, Visalia, CA

"Silhouette Special Editions are — 1.) Superb! 2.) Great! 3.) Delicious! 4.) Fantastic! . . . Did I leave anything out? These are books that an adult woman can read . . . I love them!"

—H.C.*, Monterey Park, CA

*names available on request